Elliot K. Carnucci is a Big Fat Loser

A Book About Bullying

Catherine DePino

Published by Rogue Phoenix Press

ISBN: 978-1540525123

Credits
Cover Artist: Designs by Ms G
Editor: Sherry Derr-Wille

Dedication

I dedicate this book to my dear grandchildren: Drew, Hope, Luke, Chase, and Cole. You are the sunshine of my life.

Chapter One: The Secret of the Universe

"Help—I can't breathe—let me out. Somebody help..."

I pounded the inside of the musty supply closet until my knuckles turned blue. Did anybody even have the key?

What if they don't come? What if I'm trapped here all night?

I could hear loud voices and laughing, so I knew Kyle Canfield and one of his friends from the basketball team were there, waiting to see if I would cave in and plead for mercy.

The bell blared. Classes changed. Kids stampeded through the halls. Then, silence.

Finally, I heard someone shout, "I've got the key, Doc."

"Thanks, Duke," Doc Greely, the assistant principal, said to Mr. Boardly, the man who'd sprung me loose.

Mr. Boardly, the head custodian, better known as Duke, offered me his arm, and I stumbled out of the closet. He was as thin as his mop handle, but all muscle, no flab like me. A scruffy white beard covered half his face.

He slammed the closet door shut and bolted the lock. "One of the hall guards reported noise coming from this area. We came as soon as we heard."

Duke patted my shoulder. "Let me know if I can help, Elliot." I could hear his keys clanging as he walked down the hall humming "Duke of Earl," that old sixties song he loved. That's where he got his nickname.

~ * ~

"Up to their old tricks again, Elliot?" Doc asked on the way to his office.

I figured it was a dumb question, so I looked at the ground like I always do when an adult says something stupid.

Doc walked beside me, babbling nonstop. "As I said when they pelted you with those mini pizzas in the cafeteria, 'I'll do everything I can, but I can't be there every minute.'"

The kids at Ralph Bunche High School make fun of Doc because he has a belly that flops over his belt and makes him look like he's about to have a baby. They call him "Beer Gut Greely" behind his back.

Out of the corner of my eye, I could see Kyle Canfield and his buddy Derek Parker smiling. "Fat loser," one of them whispered. That was their favorite name for me, but they loved to call me "2K," meaning two tons, so the teachers wouldn't have a clue about what they were up to.

Doc spun around to where they were standing. He enjoyed what he called "catching culprits in the act," but it was too late. Kyle and Derek had already made a mad dash down the hall.

Doc barked into his walkie-talkie to Officer Grady, the school cop. "Pick up Canfield and Parker in homeroom. Have the dean give them in-school suspension for three days. Looks like they didn't learn much from those detentions we gave them last time."

"You got it, boss," Grady shouted over the phone static.

I followed Doc to his office and sank into the butt aching folding chair he reserved for kids who talked back, cursed out teachers, or cut class. Doc leaned back in his swivel chair and tapped the tips of his fingers together.

I read in *Psychology Today* how body language can tell you what's going on in people's heads. Steepling your fingers shows you think you're better than everybody. Doc thinks he has all the answers, especially when it comes to my harassment issues.

When I thought Doc would tumble over in his chair, he braced his hands on the desk and straightened up like he had a broomstick up his butt. He pointed his finger so close to my face I thought he'd gouge out my eye and I'd have to roam the earth like a Cyclops for the rest of my life.

He leaned toward me, and I could smell the stinky salami and provolone sandwich he usually ate for lunch. "You know who can help you?"

I shrugged, knowing what his answer would be.

"*You* can help you," he said, like he was giving me the secret of the universe.

I looked at him like he was an alien, but he didn't catch it.

"What do you have to say about all this, Elliot?"

I shrugged my shoulders. What did he expect me to say, that I was the big fat loser those guys always called me?

By now the whole school knew because they'd scribbled that name and a few others I won't mention on the bathroom wall.

Doc squinted at me with his muddy hazel eyes. He hated it when you didn't answer right away.

I shifted in my seat. "For one thing, I'm not a loser like they say. Slightly unpopular maybe, but not a loser."

The *fat* part bothered me most. It's not that I haven't tried to control my appetite. I live with my dad who has a terminal weight problem, and my grandmother's force-fed me since birth.

If I don't eat, she says, "You want to grow up to be a big hulk like your father or a puny runt like the other side of the family?" She means the Kravitz side, of which my mom's a main member.

Doc raised his bushy eyebrows and shook his head like he did the other times Kyle and his boys bugged me, like he thought I was hopeless. Then he wrote a hall pass and sent me back to homeroom.

I didn't hurry because I consider homeroom the absolute worst period of the day. I say that because homeroom's nothing more than a group of kids banded together by their last names. I'm stuck with the *C's*, the biggest pains in the school, Kyle Canfield being a prime example.

In the fall, Kyle transferred here from Morgan Academy, a school for preppy kids. Not long after, Duke spotted the graffiti on the bathroom wall. Doc rounded up Kyle and his friends and made them scrub the red marker away until the wall was dingy gray again. It took hours, but they got to miss gym and health, my least favorite subjects, so it didn't seem like much of a punishment to me.

I knew Kyle must be planning something new because when I passed him on the way to my desk, he flashed me his smug smile and went back to texting his friends.

Not that I'm paranoid, but I'd seen that look before, and it always meant trouble.

His smile faded fast. Grady, the cop, breezed in and stood cross-armed at his desk. "We meet again, Canfield."

Now I was really in for it. Anytime Kyle got in trouble, he gave me twice as much back.

Chapter Two: A Wiener and Fries

To my surprise, it looked like Kyle had decided to keep a low profile after coming off suspension, except for a few muffled *2k's* when he passed me in the halls.

Maybe the threat of getting thrown off the basketball team stopped him from coming after me. I wasn't going to let my guard down because you never knew with him.

I didn't really have time to think about Kyle because during the next few days I had chorus rehearsals during lunch. We were working on show tunes for a parents' night concert, and Ms. Cooper, the choir director, gave me a solo for the third time this year.

The lyrics of the song I'd sing, "This is the Moment," from the Broadway show, "Jekyll and Hyde," hit me like a blast of sunshine.

The words made me think things might eventually work out even though it might not seem that way now. Was I kidding myself? All I knew was when I sang nothing else seemed to matter. After the kids left practice and we were alone, Ms. Cooper said, "I'm going to introduce you to one of the top singing teachers in Philly. That voice is going to take you places."

A few days after the concert, I brought my lunch tray to a corner table far from Kyle and his friends. No sooner had I sunk my fork into a plate of mushy Shepherd's Pie when *splat*, a clump of squishy mustard landed on my head.

Kyle and a couple of teammates surrounded my table, and using those packets you get with hot dogs and fries, aimed rounds of mustard, followed by ketchup, at every part of my anatomy.

When I tried to make a run for it, Kyle stuck his immense foot in my path. The kids around me couldn't see because his friends were blocking me. Not that most of them would have done anything to stop it.

Red and yellow dripped from my arms, legs, and hair, making me look like a jumbo Ronald McDonald.

I guess somebody finally noticed because before long Doc appeared on the scene with Officer Grady.

Doc nodded toward Kyle and his friends, who had almost made it to the cafeteria entrance. "Tell the dean I want them suspended, no in-school suspension this time. We'll need to see a parent before we let them back in."

"Sure thing, boss," Officer Grady said, running to catch up with them.

I dumped the plate of Shepherd's Pie in the trash. It smelled like throw up and looked like the slop they feed inmates.

Doc turned to me. "Any idea what brought this one on?"

"Maybe they were pissed because they'd lost the game to Calvin Coolidge High, and they needed to take it out on somebody. Does it really matter?"

Doc rubbed his forehead. "I guess there's never a reason, one that counts anyway. The important thing is what to do about it."

I wiped my head and arms with my sleeve but the mustard and ketchup clung to me like paint.

"I'll do what I can from my end," Doc said. "Do you have any ideas about how to stop this?"

He peered at the kids at a nearby table who had started to stare, and they turned away.

"Let's go talk in my office," Doc said, and I followed him down the hall.

Did he really expect an answer? Nobody in the school could make them stop, so what made him think I would know what to do? I didn't want to be stuck in Doc's dingy office all day, so I had to say something.

"I probably shouldn't sit by myself in the lunchroom if I don't want to be an open target. The problem is my friend Roy practices with the track team, so he can't always be here."

Doc gave me a look. "I guess you'll have to make more friends then."

"I don't have time. I'm too busy with honors classes, Mathletes, and chorus."

Had I confirmed Doc's suspicion I was a genuine geek and loser like Kyle and his friends thought?

Doc took off his glasses and rubbed his eyes. "That kind of attitude will get you nowhere. I'm not saying you have to be part of a crowd, but maybe you can meet more kids, do things together."

"I'll think about it," I said, hoping he'd stop yapping.

Doc reached for his phone. "I'll call your mother and father, tell them we need to talk."

"My parents are divorced. I live with my dad and grandmother. Mom lives in California."

"It will have to be Dad then." Doc never gave up.

"Dad probably won't be able to make it. He's a funeral director and works twenty-four/seven."

Doc ignored me and dialed our number.

Dad answered on the first ring. His voice boomed out over the receiver. Doc jerked the phone away from his ear. "Carnucci Home for Funerals. Andrew speaking. How may I help you?"

When they finished talking, Doc let out a little laugh, which is rare for him. "Your father told me more than I needed to know. He said his main assistant's at a convention, so he has to do the embalming. To top that off, Maizie, his make-up artist, called in sick, and his hairdresser's in Las Vegas marrying his third wife, so he's stuck doing everything. There's no way he can come in today."

Doc smiled at me like everything was going to be okay. "He'll send your grandmother instead."

I swallowed hard. My face must have turned red because Doc

rested his chin on his palm and studied me.

"Is something wrong, Elliot?"

"No. You'll find out when she gets here."

Doc pointed to his private bathroom. "Go clean up. We can't have you roaming through the halls looking like a Picasso painting. Make it fast. I want you here for that meeting."

I was glad I took my time because when I got back, Nonna still wasn't there. We call her that because it means *grandmother* in Italian. God forbid we'd make her feel old by calling her *Grandmom*. Doc was peering in the mirror, combing a wild strand of hair over his bald spot. When he saw me, he waddled back to his desk and pretended to fumble through some papers.

Nonna took forever to get to school because she had to take a bus, and the schedule's always messed up when it rains. She charged into the office in her yellow flowered housedress and plastic rain bonnet and shook her soggy umbrella in Doc's face.

"What kind of school do you run here, mister?" she asked, her black eyes popping out of their sockets. "I leave my grandson in your care, and he ends up looking like a wiener and fries."

Doc's lips shifted like he was going to crack up when she said *wiener*, but Nonna jabbed his ribs with her umbrella, so I guess he changed his mind.

He crossed his fingers in front of him like she was a vampire. "You need to calm down, Mrs. Carnucci."

Her voice sounded like a fingernail across a chalkboard. "You need to do your job."

I felt like running out of there.

Doc rubbed his chin. "What happened to your grandson is wrong, but it's commonplace in today's schools. It's not like in our day when the worst thing we did was throw spit balls and hide thumb tacks on chairs."

He rested his hand on Nonna's arm, but she yanked it away. "We'll do our best to ensure it doesn't happen again," he said.

Nonna gave him an evil look. "You bet your shiny, bald head it won't. If it does, you'll have to answer to me and my lawyer."

I don't think Doc realized the full impact of her threat. He hadn't seen Nonna bound into Aldo's Bar and Grill at midnight and order the 7th Street Motorcycle Club to stop all the racket or she'd take care of them herself. These beefy guys had tobacco breath and tattoos, but it didn't faze Nonna.

Nonna reached for my arm, but I broke free. "Let's go, Elliot. I've heard enough of this baloney."

She shook her finger at Doc. "You haven't heard the last of me. I'm holding you personally responsible for my grandson's safety."

Doc jumped from his seat to open the door. He looked at Nonna like he hadn't heard what she'd said. "We'll talk soon, Mrs. Carnucci. Thanks for stopping by."

"You're not welcome," she said, fastening the tie on her rain bonnet.

She stormed out of his office, and I had no choice but to follow her.

~ * ~

When Nonna and I got home, Dad was standing in the reposing room, where they lay out the dead bodies, admiring the hair and make-up job on his latest customer.

I moved close to the casket and peered in. "Didn't Mr. Luisi have white hair?"

Nonna frowned. "White, black? He's dead now. He doesn't know the difference."

Dad looked like he was in a trance. He slid Mr. Luisi's trifocals down low on his nose, like he wore them when he read the sports page on his front porch, and straightened his plaid bow tie.

"Looks like he's about to pop up and dance the Tarantella like he did at his daughter's wedding," Dad said to himself.

Nonna poked Dad's shoulder with her bony finger. His head spun around like Linda Blair in that movie, "The Exorcist."

Dad looked at me all teary eyed. I didn't know if he'd gotten emotional because of what he'd heard happened at school or if he was thrilled with the job he'd done on Mr. Luisi.

"Are you okay, son?"

Nonna slammed her head with the palm of her hand.

"If you call being abused by a pack of punks okay, he's fine."

"I'll live," I said.

She motioned for me to follow her upstairs. Dad peeled off his rubber gloves and trudged up after us.

"Sit down," Nonna said, offering me a plate of oatmeal raisin cookies. "Pour yourself a glass of milk. You'll feel better."

Nonna gave my arm a little punch. "You'll need to stand up to those guys before they give you the full treatment. Today a wiener and fries, tomorrow Stromboli."

I bit into a cookie and spit out the raisins. "It's not that easy. I'm no match for Canfield and his boys."

"Don't be a wimp. I taught you better. Act as if they don't get to you, and maybe they'll stop."

I pushed the plate of cookies away. "I'm not going to listen to this. You're always telling me what to do."

"Somebody has to," Nonna said.

Dad rummaged through the fridge, grabbed a stick of pepperoni and washed it down with diet ginger ale.

"Listen to Nonna. I did, and look how I turned out."

I let out an ear-busting burp. I knew that would get to them.

Dad settled into the kitchen chair, which was way too small for him, and mopped the sweat off his face with Nonna's fancy dishrag.

"Your mother called about one of her commercials she wants you to watch on TV."

Nonna groaned. "Never 'How are you? How's the family?' Only how wonderful she is and how producers are banging down her door to make commercials."

Dad gave her a look. "She's Elliot's mother, Ma. Show some respect."

"Like the respect she showed you when she bailed out on you four years ago?"

Dad shook his head and sighed.

I hated when Nonna bad-mouthed Mom, but Mom said stuff about her too, like how frumpy she dressed. She also loved to talk about how Nonna's stomach stuck out. I guess you could say they were even.

Ever since Mom and Dad divorced, it's been like World War III with the Kravitz's and Carnuncci's always going at it. Nobody wins, but like most adults, they're too stupid to know that.

The divorce was pretty dumb too, if you ask me. "Do you ever think about anything but work?" was Mom's line to Dad, and Dad's was, "You don't know how great you have it, Rayna. Most women would die to have your kind of life."

"True," she'd say. "They'd be in the perfect place with all the other corpses."

Now Dad and Mom have joint custody, which means I'm supposed to live with both of them equal time. Since Mom's on the road a lot with her job, they agreed it would be best for me to stay with Dad and spend time with her when she's in town.

Thinking about the divorce always gets to me, so I couldn't wait to call my friend Roy. His real name is Epifanio Arroyo. We've been friends since third grade when he moved here from San Juan, Puerto Rico. The kids at school used to tease him because he speaks with an accent. Sometimes they still do, but not as much as they bug me.

Chapter Three: Zero Tolerance

Roy answered on the first ring.

I whispered into my cell phone so Nonna wouldn't hear. She loved to listen in on my conversations. Once I heard her tell her friend, Mrs. O'Reilly, that I was madly in love with Rosalie Giordano. I was, but that was none of their business.

"Why are you whispering, El?" Roy asked. "I thought you lived with dead people. They'll never tell your secrets."

"My grandmother is totally alive, in case you haven't noticed, and it's her life's mission to know all my secrets."

Roy didn't think twice about blurting things out. "Hey, I heard what happened with the ketchup and mustard. Those guys tried that once with me, but I was lucky enough to escape."

"I'm not a track star like you. I can't shake them as fast."

"Yeah, but it's not enough to make them stop bugging me," Roy said.

"I wish we could come up with something to make them stop bothering both of us."

"Don't count on it," Roy said. "The fact is they don't like either of us. Me because I talk and look different from them..."

"And me because they think I'm totally weird."

He laughed. "Like the way you dress."

"What do you mean?"

"For one thing, that tucked-in purple shirt with the discount store pants and belt you wore today doesn't do anything for you, if you want the truth." Roy could really pile it on when he wanted to.

"I look that bad?"

"Seriously, you need to stop putting yourself down. You're doing a lot of good stuff like honor society, Mathletes, and singing."

"Yeah, but to them I'm a fat geek who lives in a funeral home.

He almost broke my eardrum with his nutty laugh. "And I'm the Cookie Monster."

Besides the fact that Roy is about six foot eight and so lanky a flimsy breeze would toss him into a somersault, the kids tease him because of his deep hoarse voice that sounds like the Sesame Street character.

"I have to tell you, El, your out-of-control hair and those thick black glasses don't help your image."

My face burned hotter than a chili pepper. I felt like hanging up on him. "Are you my friend or what?"

"What do you think?"

I didn't say anything back, and neither did he.

"Look, you had this problem back in grade school and things got better," Roy finally said.

"It didn't help that my parents gave me a goofy last name like Kravitz-Carnucci."

Roy laughed. "I remember when the teacher called roll, the kids turned around to stare at you, like they looked at me when they heard *Epifanio*. If you don't mind my asking, why did they call you that anyway?"

It seemed like I was always explaining stuff my parents did. "If you must know, Mom wanted people to know I was Jewish and Italian. When she found out the kids made fun of me, she told the teacher my name was Elliot K. Carnucci and nobody had better call me anything else, or Dad would stick them in a casket and close the lid forever."

"That is a little strange," Roy said. "I guess all parents are strange in their own way." Then he got quiet for a minute. "I hate to be the one to tell you, but I was talking to your dream girl, Rosalie. She said those guys are planning something big for you, and it won't be pretty."

How could she know that if she wasn't friends with them? Maybe she'd overheard them talking.

"Do you think she's in on it?"

"Probably not. Are you still thinking of asking her out?"

"Every guy in the school likes her. You think she'd go out with me?"

"You want the truth?"

I felt like smacking him. "I can always count on you to make me feel good."

"No offense, but I don't think you're her type."

Sometimes it was better to ignore what he said, so I changed the subject. "I've been thinking. You're a hot dresser. Want to help me do one of those makeovers like they do on TV? Maybe I'll have a chance with her."

"If you do it, do it because you want to, not for anybody else."

"I am doing it for me, so she'll like me."

Roy laughed. "Why not? That's as good a reason as any. Let's go for it."

Would a makeover help, or was I totally hopeless? My black curly hair fell down on my face, and my gut stuck out like an inner tube from eating Nonna's rigatoni.

I put my ear against the door. "Wait, Roy. I think I hear something."

"A dead body coming to life? I don't know how you can live there. See who it is."

I threw open the door. Nonna let out a shriek like an ax murderer was attacking her.

Roy laughed his head off. "What's going on? Should I call 911?"

Like everybody else, the funeral home fascinated him, but I wasn't about to give him any satisfaction.

"Gotta go. We'll talk tomorrow," I said and slammed down the phone.

Nonna charged into my room. "You nearly gave me a heart attack startling me like that. I came out of my bubble bath and passed by your room. I heard you talking and wondered who you'd be chatting with this late."

"It wasn't a girl, if that's what you're thinking."

She crossed her arms and made a face. "If it was, you wouldn't tell me, would you?"

"What do you think?" I asked, practically closing the door on her big toe.

~ * ~

The next day in school we had an assembly about the evils of bullying. Doc Greely was in charge because Principal Ríos had more important things to do like roaming the halls to corral kids cutting classes or throwing chicken fingers in the lunchroom at kids they hated for no reason.

Doc peered out at us over his wire-rimmed glasses. The mic squealed and the kids plugged their ears.

"Boys and girls, I'm sending you the message that we will no longer tolerate bullying at Ralph Bunche High School. That means zero tolerance. If we catch you teasing, abusing, or harassing your classmates in any way, you will face suspension."

You could hear a few boos and catcalls from the audience. Teachers scrambled out of their seats and stood guard in front of their homerooms. Doc's hearing wasn't the greatest, so he kept talking over the noise.

"Recently, we had an incident where some students jammed a young man into a supply closet."

A couple of kids in my homeroom looked at me and laughed.

Don't mention the mustard and ketchup, Doc, please.

"To top it off, some ingenious pranksters smothered that same classmate in condiments and ruined his clothing."

Most kids probably didn't know what condiments were unless they watched The Food Channel. Just when I thought I was home free, Kyle, who sat behind me, shoved my seat with his foot, and propelled me forward. I felt my back snap. Had he given me a whiplash? I turned around and gave him a dirty look.

"Wieners deserve mustard and ketchup," he said loudly enough for everyone to hear.

A couple of kids in my homeroom hooted.

Doc's voice blasted through the microphone. Had he finally heard?

"I want you to quiet down. Teachers, if you see someone in your group misbehaving, send the student to my office."

Suddenly, everyone got quiet. They knew how long Doc's lectures could last once he got warmed up. Once he babbled on for forty-five minutes about the evils of rock star t-shirts and rap music lyrics. They had to ring the bell three times to wake up all the kids who'd dozed off.

"I need you to go to the office, Kyle," Ms. Begley, my homeroom teacher, said in her I-mean-business voice.

He took his time moving, so she motioned for Mr. Popov, the security guard standing near the stage like a mummy.

Mr. Popov was about a hundred years old and looked like he could be one of Dad's customers. He crept to the end of the aisle and stood there with his arms crossed.

"Get a move on, young man. You don't want to get into any more trouble, do you?"

Canfield narrowed his eyes at Mr. Popov. "Don't threaten me, Grandpop. I've got my rights."

Canfield stepped on my foot on the way out. "Catch you later, 2K."

Doc finally stopped yammering and told everyone to return to second period. The band started playing "It's a Grand Old Flag" like they always do when assembly's over.

Doc karate chopped the air. "Cut that blasted music," he said to Mr. Pavlova, the band director. "I'm addressing a serious problem in our school, and you're playing like it's a pep rally."

"Sor-*ry*," the band director said.

~ * ~

Later that day, I waited in the lunch line for Miss Mabel to dish out a Sloppy Joe platter.

"From now on, one ketchup and mustard to a customer," she shouted. "Some kids in this school don't know how to behave. Must have been raised in a barn."

I heard whinnying and neighing in the background, but I didn't turn around.

I took my money out of my backpack to pay, and I found a note. Who had put it there? What was it about? I stuck the paper in my pocket and rested my tray on an empty table.

Where was Roy? He usually got here first so he'd have time to eat two lunches and three fudge pops.

As it turned out, I sat by myself the whole period. Roy showed up five minutes before the bell rang and started stuffing his face with Miss Mabel's slimy spaghetti and smelly garlic bread. I could barely make out what he was saying.

He wiped his mouth on his sleeve. "Sorry I'm late. Had to meet coach to set up a practice schedule. Once it starts, I won't have time for lunch."

"Hey, don't worry. I'm used to it." I thought of all the days I'd have to eat alone.

"I'm not deserting you, buddy. There's still the phone, texting, and weekends."

Roy was packing it in so fast he started choking. I gave him a couple of forceful whacks on the back, and the spaghetti flew out of his mouth like red, slippery worms. A few kids at the next table cracked up.

He caught his breath and slurped some chocolate milk. "Don't forget we're going shopping this weekend. I'll take you to my Uncle Pablo's first. He's the hair-cutting king. Forget those uncool barber shops."

I dug into the whipped cream on top of my pea-green gelatin dessert. "The guy who does my hair, Mario, the singing barber, moonlights at my dad's place. Most of his customers are dead, but Dad forces me to go to him because he owes him for helping out. Then he gives him a fat tip for making me look ugly."

Roy burst out with his Cookie Monster laugh. "No wonder your hair looks like one of those old opera singers."

He stuck his thumb in the air. "Uncle Pablo's going to transform you into a new man."

"As long as he doesn't chop all my hair off like he did yours."

Roy rubbed his naked scalp. "I asked him to give me a close cut. It's cooler when I run."

"Have to go," I said. "We're having a test on Edgar Allan Poe in honors English, and Ms. Williams deducts points if we're late."

~ * ~

The interesting thing about living in my house is you never know what you'll face when you get home from school each day. I wondered if Roy felt the same way about his family, or if anyone else did, for that matter.

Today was no different. I found Nonna lying on a beach chair in the backyard in the icy wind, tanning herself with her friend, Mrs. O'Reilly. Her blue-white hair was set in foam rollers that made her look like an outer space creature. She had on her pink Capri pants and Dad's bowling shirt, which dwarfed her scrawny body. "Carnucci's Home for Funerals" was plastered on the back.

"Better stay out of your dad's way," Nonna said, "He's jittery as a cat getting ready for the Luisi funeral."

She grinned at Mrs. O'Reilly. What were they up to now?

"I took another peek at the body," Nonna whispered. "This time Mrs. O'Reilly came along."

Mrs. O'Reilly popped her head up from her blanket. She turned the dial on Nonna's boom box until "Boogie Woogie Bugle Boy" blared from the speaker.

Nonna's friend chuckled. "Wait 'til Viola sees her husband. He looks like an Adams family re-run with that hair, dark as tar and slicked down flat, nothing like he did in life. He was such a handsome man with that wavy, white mane."

Nonna made a face at Mrs. O'Reilly. "He looks like Rudy Giuliani, the former mayor of New York, if you ask me. You don't know the pains my son goes through to please his customers. He's an artist."

Mrs. O'Reilly raised her eyebrow. "If you say so."

Nonna grabbed her beach towel and marched toward the house. Mrs. O'Reilly scurried after her.

"I didn't mean anything by it, Angela," Mrs. O'Reilly said. "Let's not ruin our friendship over a dead man's bad hair day."

Nonna was already at the backdoor, probing the lock with her key. I raced past her up the steps to my room. I was dying to see what was in the note someone had jammed in my backpack.

Chapter Four: The Coolest Guy in the Class

That night after dinner, I dug the note out of my pocket and tore open the envelope. Expensive perfume like Mom wears, a sweet musky smell, oozed from the pink paper. The dots on the *i's* were shaped like hearts and the *o's* had smiley faces inside.

Dear Elliot,

I'm writing to ask if you want to go to a movie with some friends and me. I think you're the coolest guy in the class and the smartest. I figured you were too shy to ask me, so I'm asking you. E-mail me at this address: sweetasarose@newmail.com

Rosalie, the prettiest girl in the class, was asking me to the movies? I read the letter again to be sure I wasn't hallucinating.

I locked my door before Nonna could interrupt. I didn't have to worry about Dad because the Luisi family was starting to arrive in full force for the viewing.

I opened my shade a crack and saw Mrs. Luisi clutching her brother Carmine's arm as she struggled up the path to our house. Aunts, uncles and a hoard of cousins followed. Each Luisi sister and brother must have had ten kids apiece, but Mrs. Luisi only had her husband.

I took out my Smartphone to e-mail Rosalie, but my hands were so shaky I could hardly spell. I told Rosalie I'd like to go to the movies with her and her friends. Here's how I ended the e-mail:

Let's talk tomorrow. I'll meet you at your locker after school.

The problem was I didn't know how to sign it. *Love, Elliot* would sound too pushy. I settled for *El*, even though Roy was the only one who called me that. I'd no sooner sent the e-mail than I heard someone pounding on my door.

Dressed in her black suit and chapel veil, Nonna looked like the Wicked Witch of the West. She latched on to my hand so hard I thought she'd break my bones. "Hear that commotion down there? It sounds like Happy Hour at Aldo's Bar."

I moved toward the winding staircase and heard shouting, but I couldn't make out the words.

"Let's go investigate," Nonna said, tossing her half-finished crossword puzzle on my bed.

We got there just in time to see Mrs. Luisi push her way in front of Dad. She looked like she was going to scratch his eyes out with her pointy red nails.

"You made my husband look hideous. Everyone knew him as a handsome man with elegant silver hair. What possessed you to dye it black and slick it back like a bad Elvis impersonator? I should sue you for malpractice."

Dad rubbed his head. "All due apologies, Mrs. Luisi, but in the picture you gave me, your husband had dark hair. I thought you wanted him to look like he did in his younger years."

Mrs. Luisi started to blubber like a baby. I guess grief can do that to you. "You knew his hair had turned white. What were you thinking?'

Before Dad had a chance to answer, Mrs. Luisi's brother Carmine, who looked like a sumo wrestler, grabbed Dad's arm with his beefy hand.

"When I die, Carnucci, I won't call you. I'll take my business to Shanahan's across the street."

"That's your decision, but you must know I had the highest regard for Mr. Luisi," Dad said, trying to break away from Carmine. "I would never disrespect him or your family."

Carmine's voice boomed louder than thunder. "So what are you going to do about it?"

"Tell you what," Dad said, "I'll knock off the cost of the hair and makeup…"

Carmine squeezed Dad's arm tighter.

Dad gulped. "And discount the casket too."

I could see the vein in Nonna's neck pulsing. "Maybe I should call the cops."

Carmine let go of Dad's arm. "Can you live with that, Viola?"

Mrs. Luisi dried her eyes with her sleeve. Her mascara had zigzagged a lightning bolt across her puffy cheeks. "We'll talk about it," she said in a whiny voice. "If I'm not satisfied, I'll have to take action."

"You won't need to do that," Dad said, ushering Mrs. Luisi and her brother into a conference room.

I could see Dad was trying hard to please them, but sweat had begun to bubble around his collar, and he was breathing hard. That was the story of Dad's life. He always did his best, but sometimes he tried too hard. Every so often, it blew up in his face, like it did this time, and he couldn't figure out why.

Dad could handle all the other stuff his other workers did, but hair was one thing he didn't have a clue about. It really bothered him because he was a guy who wanted to make everything perfect for the dead people's relatives. When they weren't satisfied, he'd talk about it for days until Nonna told him to give it a rest, nobody's perfect after all.

Why couldn't he think about all the good things he did for people? He got lots of calls and e-mails from families who told him he'd made the worst day of their lives more bearable. In fact, people were always inviting him to their houses for dinner, and he even got the community service award from the Rotary Club. He keeps the plaque on his wall. I wish he'd look at it once in a while.

When things like this happen, I think the job is starting to affect his health, so a few days ago I asked him about it. "Why don't you leave? You could do something else, sell cars or manage a restaurant..."

He shrugged. "My family would never forgive me if Carnucci's got gobbled up by the big funeral chains. Before my dad died, I promised to carry on his legacy."

Was that why he went out of his way to make things perfect and why he was trying now to make things right with the Luisis? I wanted to believe it was that and not Carmine's swift wrestling moves.

Most of the guests pretended not to hear the family yelling at Dad, but the Luisi grandkids, who went to my school, laughed so hard I thought they'd pee on the reposing room floor. I was sure everyone at school would hear the whole story the next day.

~ * ~

When I got back to my room, my answering machine was blinking like crazy. I pressed the play button, and I heard Mom's frantic voice.

"Elliot, my plane just got in. I'll be in town for a few days doing a commercial for false teeth dancing around in a glass. What is my life coming to? I'll meet you at the front gate after school tomorrow, and we'll grab an early dinner.

The next day, Mom was waiting for me in her rental car, a pale blue Mercedes convertible. She had on leggings, a black leather skirt, and a flowered shirt. Her sleek auburn hair was pulled up in a bun. She'd call it a *chignon*.

I moved the seat back so I wouldn't feel smooshed. "Can we get pizza?"

"Sounds good, as long as we don't order pepperoni like we did last time. I can't afford to gain weight in my business, and neither can you, for that matter. By the way, your dad tells me you're taking singing lessons."

"My teacher says I can sing professionally when I get older. I think he just wants our money."

Mom shook her finger at me. "Don't put yourself down, Elliot. You'll never get ahead that way."

She was probably right. Maybe that was one of the reasons those guys bugged me like they did. I needed to upgrade my image, inside and out.

After dinner, Mom dropped me off home. "I'll pick you up after school again tomorrow, and we'll hang out."

I wanted to see Mom. She hadn't been home in two months, but all I could think of was how I'd have to rush if I was going to meet Rosalie at her locker.

Even worse, what would I say to Rosalie? I'd never talked to her in person, except for the time I'd accidentally tripped her when she was my line-dancing partner in gym. I'd helped her up, and she'd said, "No problem," and went on dancing even though a kid who'd noticed called me *Elliot Klutz Loser*.

The whole time I was with Mom I couldn't stop thinking about the letter Rosalie sent. I was itching to get home, and I was glad when Mom said how beat she was and took me home early instead of talking endlessly about her latest trip to LA.

~ * ~

The first thing I did when I got home from Mom's was to call Roy with the good news.

My words spilled out. "You won't believe this..."

"Let me guess. You got up the nerve to ask Rosalie to the movies."

"Close. She asked *me*."

Roy erupted into his goofy laugh. "Get serious. Rosalie wouldn't ask you to go out with her. Maybe she did it on a dare, or as a joke."

Why did he have to act like he knew it all?

"If that's true, why would she give me her e-mail address?"

"You're too quick to believe everything you hear. That's why those guys mess with you."

Could Roy be right? After all, he was used to kids messing with him.

"You think this is some kind of trick?"

I didn't hear anything on the other end. "Roy, you still there?"

"I'm saying you have to question things. If somebody like Rosalie asks you to the movies, you have to wonder if it's true."

My body felt as heavy as my voice. "Thanks. I knew you'd be happy for me."

Roy was a good friend, but he could also be a pain.

"I'm on your side, buddy."

"It doesn't seem that way."

I felt like hanging up on him, but I knew it would make things worse.

Roy shot back at me with his know-it-all voice. "Think about it. You hardly know Rosalie. Why would she ask you, especially when all the popular guys like her? My guess is that one of them has already asked her. Maybe even..."

"Don't say it. I know what you're thinking."

"It's all around school that Canfield has his eye on her."

I felt a sour taste in my mouth. "You think he'd have a chance with her?"

Roy chuckled. "Compared to you, probably."

"I don't appreciate your insults."

"You're too sensitive, El, and that's not fun."

I'd just about had about all I could take from him. "If you don't want to hang out with me, let me know."

"There you go again."

I knew one of us had to stop, or we'd keep spinning in circles. This time, I knew it had to be me.

"Forget it. Why are we arguing?"

"For once, I agree." Roy paused. "Next time you talk to Rosalie, ask her if she has a friend. We can double date."

Was he serious? "No chance. You wouldn't be her type."

He let out his wacky laugh, but I hung up before he could say anything.

Chapter Five: Lots of Favor

I got back my Poe test on 'The Tell Tale Heart' with a note from Ms. Williams. "Elliot, this gives me goose bumps."

I hid my paper so no one would see.

"The Tell Tale Heart" is my favorite Poe story. It's about this guy who murders a man and hides his body under the floor. He keeps hearing the man's heart beat and can't do anything to stop it.

Ms. Williams knelt by my desk the way waiters do to make you like them so you'll give them a fat tip.

"How would you feel about reading your essay to the class?"

"I'd rather not," I said, slinking down in my chair.

I heard a few snickers from the back of the room. This was the first time my honors class had ragged on me, but I wasn't surprised because Kyle recently transferred to all my classes. His parents think he's a genius, and they probably bugged the principal until she gave in and put him in all the top classes.

Kyle had most of the teachers conned. For one thing, our journal project for Ms. Williams was due last week. I heard him telling her he had the stomach virus and had spent the whole day in the bathroom, which might have been believable if Roy hadn't spotted him at the video arcade around the time he was supposed to be puking his guts out.

Roy and I couldn't believe how Ms. Williams gave him an extra week for the project. She definitely wasn't what you'd call a pushover. But Kyle knew how to get his way, how to make lies sound like the truth so no one would question him.

When he finally turned in the journal, Ms. Williams gave him a cold look. "Glad to see you're better, Kyle, but don't use that excuse again. It won't work."

Somebody may have clued her in. Could Roy have whispered in her ear? He usually didn't rat out people, but Kyle was a special case.

"It's okay, Elliot. I'll get someone else to read today," Ms. Williams said. She knew about my situation and probably didn't want to push things.

Kyle leaned over my desk. "Come on, Carnucci," he called out. "Read your essay. You know everything about dead people. After all, you live in a funeral parlor."

"*Home*," I said.

Kyle smirked. "Is there a difference?"

Ms. Williams moved toward Kyle's desk and stared him down.

"If you change your mind, Elliot, let me know." She fixed her eyes on Kyle. "Meanwhile, I'll post it online with some other good ones."

When Ms. Williams turned to write our vocabulary words on the board, Kyle tapped me on the shoulder.

"Yo, Elliot, I'm busy with practice. Have a big game this weekend. I need you to write my poem for English."

I didn't bother turning around, but I could feel his cigarette breath on my face.

"It's due Monday. I'll be lucky if I can finish my own."

"You'll find a way. Meet me at my locker before first period Monday. Don't let anybody see you giving it to me."

"I'll see what I can do," I said.

Lately, he'd been asking me for lots of favors. I was beginning to feel like I didn't have a choice. Maybe if I gave in, he'd stop bugging me.

When I told Roy about it, he said I was asking for more trouble and that I should stand up to Kyle. Wouldn't that make things worse?

The bell rang, and I raced like a gazelle to my next class, which was on the other side of the building. Mr. Taylor, my math teacher, made you do twenty push-ups for every minute you were late. I'm not in the best shape, so I ran like crazy to beat the bell.

~ * ~

Mr. Taylor licked his index finger and counted out algebra tests for each row.

"I hope everyone studied," Mr. Taylor said. "This test is a killer, tough enough to make the Mathletes sweat."

He looked straight at me, but impossible math tests are my specialty. I'd much rather take them than fitness tests in gym, which I almost failed last time. They had this wicked obstacle course where you had to climb ropes and jump over wooden horses, which isn't easy if you've packed on extra pounds.

Halfway through the test, Kyle, who sat next to me in math, coughed.

I tried to ignore him, but he coughed again, and I didn't want Mr. Taylor to think I was cheating.

He formed the words with his mouth. "Numbers seven and ten." He could have made a bundle as a ventriloquist. Teachers never caught him asking for answers.

He knew how to get on the good side of Mr. Taylor, the hardest teacher in the school. I couldn't believe Mr. Taylor couldn't see through him. Once when Kyle didn't do his homework, Kyle told him his dog had to be put to sleep and he was too depressed to do any work. Mr. Taylor actually fell for it. I guess Ms. Williams hadn't clued him in yet.

I pretended I didn't hear Kyle asking for answers. When Mr. Taylor turned to answer the phone, Kyle stretched his rubbery neck over my desk and copied my answers. Did I have a choice?

He gave my arm a sharp jab. "I owe you one, Carnucci."

I felt my heart beating fast. I had to hold myself back from punching him. "No. I owe *you* one."

His lips formed a straight line, and he narrowed his eyes. "What's that supposed to mean?"

I looked past him. "Nothing."

"Time's up," Mr. Taylor said. "Pass your papers to the front."

~ * ~

After class, I took my time going to lunch, knowing Roy would be at track practice. It wasn't fun eating alone, so I looked around for someone to sit with.

There's this guy, LeBron Mickens, in my honors classes who keeps to himself. He'd rather read than make small talk.

The other kids respect his privacy and don't mess with him. It helps that he's a muscular giant who wears a do-rag. As usual, his head was buried in a book.

"Hi," I said, approaching his table with my tray. "Anybody sitting here?"

"You are," he said closing his book.

He looked up at me. "Ever read *The Catcher in the Rye*? It's about this kid, Holden Caufield, who's in a mental hospital. The whole book is about him telling his shrink how he ended up there."

"Haven't read it yet, but I plan to."

I sat down and started chomping on Miss Mabel's version of spaghetti and meatballs. Nonna would have trashed it, but when I'm starved, I'll eat anything, even if the meatballs taste hard as hockey pucks and the pasta sauce gels like coagulated blood. I washed down the pasta with lemonade. "Why did the guy in the book wind up in a mental hospital?"

LeBron's deep, dark eyes looked right through you. "'Cause he took things too hard, let other people rule his life. For instance, he worried his little sister would see the nasty words on the school wall. He tried to erase them but couldn't. He let everything get to him, and that's what ruined him."

I put my fork down. "You think if you let people get to you, you might end up like him?"

"That's exactly what I'm saying. Might be none of my business, but from what I can see, all that grief Kyle and his boys give you is doing you in."

"Looks like everyone in school knows."

LeBron nodded. "It's pretty obvious. It doesn't have to be that way."

"Is that why you don't hang out with other kids, why you'd rather be alone?"

He eased his book into his backpack. "No, I prefer being alone. Anyway, do I look like somebody they'd mess with?"

My eyes swept over his gigantic shoes and his hulk-like arms. "I don't think so."

He smiled. "Fact is, I like to figure out what's going on in people's heads without even knowing them, like I did with you just now."

I didn't know whether to say "thanks" or "butt out," so I didn't say anything.

After a few minutes, I got up to leave, and I saw Canfield and his boys moving toward my table, so I moved quickly.

I sped out into the hall and LeBron caught up with me. "Hey, slow down, man. Why are you running? If they know they're getting to you, they'll bug you more. Canfield always has a strategy."

I eased my pace and walked beside him. "Why do you say that?"

"Canfield's a pro at bullying 'cause he's had a lot of practice. He knows what moves to make to get to you."

"How do you know so much about him?"

"Went to King Elementary with him. Even back in the fourth and fifth grade, he wanted to have a following and show he was in charge. Guess it made him feel big and bad to pick on a kid who wasn't in the in-crowd. He did the same thing he does now, targeted one kid at a time, usually someone he thought wouldn't fight back and someone he knew wouldn't tell on him."

"Didn't he ever get in trouble?"

"Once in a while, but they never did anything big to him, just gave him warnings or detentions, or called his home. Canfield was shrewd and did things under cover so no one would catch him. His dad always bailed him out just like he does now."

"How did he end up here?"

"His parents transferred him to Morgan Academy, thinking a private school would help straighten him out, but he picked on kids there too, so they kicked him out. Then we got lucky."

All of a sudden I felt cold. "Only now he's more dangerous because he's had tons of practice, and he's older and meaner."

LeBron looked over at Kyle who was sweet-talking a couple of girls by his locker. "You've got that right. He knows how to play the system and sweet talk his teachers. As my grandma would say, 'He rules the roost.' His crowd will do whatever he says because he knows how to pull their strings. If they don't go along with him, they'll be out in the cold."

It amazed me how LeBron could look at people and figure them out. "You should be a psychiatrist," I said.

He smiled. "Don't need to be a shrink to figure him out. If it wasn't you, he'd find somebody else to pick on. He'll do whatever it takes to make himself look powerful in front of his buddies."

Somehow, Canfield ended up near me. He craned his gangly neck to hear our conversation.

"Maybe you could come to my house some time," LeBron said. "I live down the road from your place. I saw you get off the bus."

"I thought you didn't like hanging out with people."

"That's most people. You're different."

I stopped at my locker and grabbed my books for my next class. "That's what they tell me."

LeBron shook his head. "Not what I meant. I hear what you say in English class. You think a lot like I do. Sometime I'd like to talk to you, get your take on things."

I found myself smiling. "I'd like that."

I hoped I hadn't sounded too anxious, like I didn't have any friends.

I couldn't wait for school to be over. Would Rosalie be there like she'd said? If she showed up, what would I say to her? How would I stall Mom from coming into school and seeing us together?

~ * ~

After school I raced to my locker before Mom had the chance to show up. I was huffing and puffing, and the sweat was pouring off me like the time I'd helped Dad lug those clunky mahogany caskets into the showroom.

I stuck my nose under my armpits to see if I smelled. I didn't, but I sneaked into the boys' room to smear on deodorant, just in case. I always kept some in my backpack. I didn't want Kyle and his friends to have one more thing to bug me about.

When I came out, Rosalie was waiting for me at my locker. What was Kyle doing there? Could they have planned this ahead of time?

I turned to Kyle. "What are you...?" The words stuck in my throat.

He shrugged. "I wanted to see what Rosalie has to say about her e-mail to you."

"I didn't e-mail him," Rosalie said. She turned toward Kyle. "I thought you asked me here to..."

My face felt like it was on fire. I turned to Rosalie, but she kept her eyes on Kyle.

"I don't understand any of this, and I don't think I want to," she said.

Two of Canfield's friends, Jason Bristow and Derek Parker, popped up from around the corner. They had on their basketball uniforms, and Jason was dribbling his ball all over the hallway like he thought he was an NBA star.

Kyle put his hand on Rosalie's shoulder, but she backed away. "2K actually thinks you and your friends would go to the movies with him."

Jason and Derek nudged each other.

Rosalie gave Kyle and his friends a disgusted look and stormed off.

The full force of Canfield's tricks, like the fake e-mail from Rosalie and staging the meeting at my locker, hit me like a sucker punch. I suddenly forgot about everything Mahatma Gandhi and Martin Luther King preached about taking the path of least resistance.

I moved toward Kyle. "I'm not taking this anymore."

His friends grinned at each other.

Canfield threw me a sarcastic smile. "You want to fight me?"

In an instant, I felt a rush of power surge through my body. I aimed for his perfect nose.

Bristow and Parker grabbed me around the waist. My arms went limp under their steely grip.

The next thing I heard was Duke's keys jangling from the chain on his waist as he ambled down the hall. "Rosalie came and got me 'cause Doc Greely was at a meeting."

My face felt hot and my eyes burned. I wanted to get out of there fast.

Kyle and his friends raced toward the door. "Whoa, not so fast..." Duke said, holding up his hand.

Canfield moved in close to me. He reeked of sweat. "You're so dumb you can't tell a fake e-mail address. Who'd believe somebody as cool as Rosalie would call herself *sweetasarose*?"

Duke's voice was as thick as gravel. "Stop this now, or we'll fix your tails good. I didn't see what happened, but I can imagine."

Those guys took off like someone had thrown kerosene on them and lit a match.

Duke coughed and wiped his mouth with a checkered handkerchief.

"They're on you every chance they get, aren't they? We've got to find a way to get them to stop."

I wiped the sweat off my face with my jacket. "Have any ideas?"

"Matter of fact, I do. We'll talk soon. I'll also let Doc know what happened so he can keep on top of this. Meanwhile, try to stay cool."

He pulled an inhaler from his pocket, tossed his head back, and sprayed. "What was the fight about?"

I didn't want to tell him about Rosalie, but I felt I owed him some explanation after he'd helped me.

"Those guys set me up, and I lost control."

"It was about a girl, wasn't it?"

Before I could answer, Mom breezed in. She was wearing rhinestone-studded jeans and a sparkly spandex top. Her long reddish hair cascaded down her neck like she was Queen Nefertiti.

"Elliot, why do you look so disheveled? Did something happen with those boys your father told me about?"

Why did she always have to embarrass me and treat me like I was in elementary school?

"I've got it under control, Mom. I don't want to talk about it."

Duke held out his hand, and Mom shook it.

"William Walker Boardly, school custodian. There was almost a fight here, but things have calmed down for now. I was about to tell your son not to stay in the building any longer than he has to."

Mom chewed on her lower lip. "Please call me Rayna. Thanks for helping my son. Is there anything I can do? I know I'm not as available as his father, but I want to help."

"Feel free to call me Duke."

He started hacking again. I thought he was going to choke on his own saliva.

Mom rummaged through her silver tote bag and offered him a cough drop, but he waved it away. "It's going to take more than that to cure what's ailing me, but thanks. Getting back to Elliot, we'll all work together, but he has to tell us when those boys give him trouble."

"I'm not going to tell on them. I can handle it," I said, but I wondered how much longer I could go on without getting into another fight.

Duke lowered his voice. "We all need support sometimes, son."

Mom took a tissue from her purse and dabbed her eyes. "I don't want you to wait until it's too late. We can only guess what they're capable of."

Duke wrote something on a piece of paper and handed it to Mom. "If you need to reach me, here's my number. We all look out for one another here."

She put the paper in her wallet. "Thanks."

After he left, she put her arm around me. "I know you don't think so now, but it's going to get better, maybe not right away, but eventually."

I broke away from her grasp. "It's a lot more complicated than that, Mom. You don't know."

I could see little lines under her eyes that hadn't been there before.

Her voice broke. "Talk to me, and we'll figure out what to do."

"Let's get out of here," I said, bracing my backpack on my shoulders. "I have a ton of homework."

She looked at her watch and frowned. "I didn't realize it was so late. Come on, I'll drop you off home. I have an appointment with my agent this afternoon, so I have to hustle. We'll hang out tomorrow instead."

I stared at the dingy blue wall. "I guess we'll have that talk later when you're not busy."

She gave me a frosty stare. "Don't make me feel guilty. I have to make a living, but that doesn't mean I don't have time for you."

Sometimes I felt like I was the parent. Just when I thought she wanted to help, she'd back off. Every time.

Chapter Six: Something to Tell You

Mom had the top down on her car that afternoon even though the March wind blew cold and frosty, but I didn't mind. The sunshine made me feel better.

She didn't say much on the ride home other than ask the usual questions about Dad and Nonna: Does Dad do anything other than talk about his customers and polish his caskets so you can see your face in them? Is he dating anyone? Is Nonna still cooking those fattening dinners that clog up your arteries? Is she still addicted to bingo at Holy Angels Church?

She pulled up in front of the Carnucci Home for Funerals sign. "Now that you're taking singing lessons, why don't you try out for the school musical? Your teacher says you have the best voice in chorus."

"I'll think about it, but the same kids usually get the parts."

"At least try. If I'd pushed harder, I'd be starring in a soap opera by now."

A tear messed up her mascara. I hated when she got emotional. "Make the most of your singing talents, Elliot, so you don't have to settle for second best like I did."

Mom was always crying or laughing about something. One day she was the queen of commercials, getting the break of a lifetime and making big money, and the next, she was locked up in her apartment, complaining how she'd soon be a homeless person if she didn't get more jobs.

I hated to see her that way, but I had enough stuff to think about with Kyle on my back. Besides, wasn't she supposed to be the parent?

Mom reached over and messed up my hair like she did when I was little. "I'll pick you up around dinner time tomorrow. I have something to tell you."

"What is it?" I asked. She was always springing stuff on me.

"I'll tell you when I see you tomorrow." She gave her horn a loud honk and waved at me.

I raced up to my room. I hoped Dad and Nonna hadn't heard me come in.

I looked at my phone because Roy had started texting me:

What happened?

Not much.

She changed her mind?

It wasn't her.

I knew it.

Canfield. Yeah I give up.

Don't!

See ya.

~ * ~

Mom strolled in after dinner while we were eating Nonna's famous fudge cake with buttercream icing and rainbow sprinkles.

"Hello, Rayna. You look lovely," Dad said, wiping the creamy frosting from his lips.

You could tell he still had a thing for Mom. There was no way she'd give up her movie star life to live among the dead, as she called it, or put up with Nonna butting into her life.

"Thanks, Andrew. I just came from an audition, can you believe, for dentures? Looking at those false teeth chattering in a coffee mug makes me want to barf."

Nonna started laughing so hard she choked, and little particles of cake sprayed across the table.

Dad gave her his version of the Heimlich, but she shoved him out of the way, and he fell to the floor.

"Easy, Ma," he said, struggling to get up. "That self-defense course you're taking is turning you into Tarzan."

Mom picked up the chair Dad toppled over. "If I'd known I'd cause this much trouble, I would have told Elliot to meet me at my place."

My voice came out loud and pleading. "Can you guys stop?"

"Don't strain your voice, son," Dad said, scrambling up from the floor. "You have a singing lesson tomorrow."

He quit rubbing his butt and put his arm around me.

"They don't mean anything by it. You know that, don't you?"

"Yeah, right," I said, and followed Mom out the door.

~ * ~

As soon as we got in the car, Mom turned the car radio to her cool rock station. She rolled down the window even though snow flurries flew in our faces.

When we got to her apartment, the first thing I noticed were those cardboard boxes they pack produce in at the grocery store. She'd loaded them with books, papers, and her antique doll collection.

"What's all this?" I asked, flopping down on her white rattan sofa. "Are you having a garage sale? Why would you get rid of your best stuff?"

She sat down across from me in her favorite white wicker papa san chair, which made her look small and helpless like a child. She reached over and touched my hand.

"I know this is sudden, and I didn't want to spring it on you, but I got an offer in LA to do a sitcom pilot. It's about a single mom who gets her big break as a rock star. I'll be staying longer than usual this time."

I looked down at the pink and teal Persian rug. The hearts and stars on the rug started swirling together until I thought my brain would crack.

She reached for my hand. "Be happy for me, Elliot. This is the chance I've dreamed of all my life."

I tried to sound like I didn't care, but I could feel my heart drop. "When are you leaving?"

"Soon. They're giving me time to wrap things up here. I'll send you a round trip ticket to LA once I'm settled. Of course I'll come back and visit. We can stay at one of those fancy hotels in center city where they have a doorman."

"Nonna's right," I said.

"What do you mean?"

"It's always about you and how wonderful you are."

"She said that?"

The vein near her eye twitched. "I guess I'm not surprised."

I fished my cell phone out of my pocket. "You don't have to drive me home. I'll call Dad."

"Why are you acting this way? Talk to me," she said in her most pitiful voice.

I ignored her and pulled my cell phone out of my pocket and dialed our number.

He answered in his funeral director's voice. "Carnucci Home for Funerals. This is Andrew."

I tried to sound normal so he wouldn't hear how down I felt. "Can you pick me up?"

"Now? Why not stay at your mother's like you've planned? Wanda Grindle's on the other line. She wants her father to be buried in his Cadillac with the top down. Can you believe it? This business gets more bizarre each day. Have to go, son."

I hung up without saying good-bye, but I don't think he noticed.

The next morning Mom made pancakes, bacon, and home fries for breakfast, which she hasn't done since I was in first grade. The potatoes didn't taste the same. I shoved them to the side of my plate.

"Why'd you put onions in them? You know I hate them."

"You always liked them that way," she said, looking like I'd told her I hated her and not the potatoes.

Chapter Seven: Trashed

On the way to school Monday, Mom turned the radio up full blast. "Brown Eyed Girl," an old Van Morrison song, was playing and she started singing off-key.

She pulled up in front of the building where kids were racing to get to class before the second bell rang.

She turned the radio off and reached over to touch my shoulder. "We'll talk more. I'll call you tomorrow."

I pulled away from her and slammed the car door. "I'd rather you didn't."

A couple of Kyle's friends hanging around the school entrance gawked at me as I passed the Ralph Bunche statue.

"Yo, 2K," Jason asked. "Have a fight with Mommy?"

Derek elbowed him. "Heard she hated living in the funeral home. Did she want to escape from you or the dead bodies?"

I hurried to the side entrance so I wouldn't have to pass those guys.

As I ran to my locker, I remembered Kyle had said to meet him with that poetry assignment. Would I be able to avoid him? Giving in was getting me nowhere. I had to try something different to get him off my back, but what?

Before I had time to think, I felt his grip on my arm.

"Have that poem? I need it now so I can recopy it."

"I didn't have time. Too busy this weekend."

He stared me down. "If you know what's good for you, you'll do what I say."

I took a breath. "What if I don't?"

He looked at me like I was a spider he was about to smash.

I grabbed my English book from the locker and held on to my loose-leaf binder that had the poem I'd written for the assignment. There was no way he was going to take it from me.

His voice had an edge to it. "You'll pay for this."

My heart started racing, and an acidy taste backed up in my throat. "Why don't you back off, Kyle?"

"Because you're a big, fat loser. Lots of kids think so except maybe your amigo Arroyo. That's only 'cause he's desperate for friends."

He spat a blob of slimy spit on my suede shoe. I rubbed my foot against the floor, but couldn't get the spot off no matter how hard I tried.

I slammed my locker. I could feel my fists tightening, itching to make contact with Kyle's face. If I punched him, I'd get suspended, maybe even arrested, so I inhaled slowly, exhaled, and walked away.

A bunch of kids rushed by on their way to class. It looked like I was becoming invisible again, but in a different sense. A lot of kids knew what was going on, but they weren't about to get involved. I guess Kyle's reputation as a guy you shouldn't mess with had a lot to do with it.

~ * ~

The first person I saw when I got to social studies was Rosalie. I eased into the desk next to her.

She sat in the back row and wore a white sun visor with gold glitter even though it wasn't officially spring yet. None of the teachers bugged her about wearing a hat in the building like they did the other kids. Not only was she a genius in math and science, but she also had a way of making teachers like her without acting like a kiss up.

Not that everyone thought she was perfect like I did. I once heard a couple of girls in our class say she was a snob because she didn't mingle much, but I never saw it that way. I think she was just kind of shy. Could they have been jealous because all the guys loved her?

She leaned toward me. My heart flopped down to my butt.

"I didn't have anything to do with the letter those guys sent you. Kyle asked me to meet at your locker while he apologized for the mustard and ketchup. I guess he wanted me to think he had a heart, and I was gullible enough to fall for it. It's all around school that we made a fool of you. Sorry."

I lowered my voice so no one would hear. "Maybe what happened isn't so bad because I got to talk to you. I'd like to be friends."

"Okay," she said.

Was she just being polite or did she mean it?

I looked at her green eyes with those long lashes, and I felt like I was channeling a different person, somebody like Canfield, who knew what he wanted and always got it.

The kid who sat in the seat next to her crouched over me with his arms folded. I scrambled out of his seat and made my way to my own desk.

Nonna says when something good happens like it did when I got to talk to Rosalie, something bad happens to balance it out. I'm usually not taken in by superstitious stuff, but somehow I felt jumpy and couldn't concentrate in my next class.

~ * ~

I was on my way to lunch that day when I heard a loud, scraping noise from down the hall. Before I had a chance to turn around to see what was going on, a pair of burly arms grabbed me and hurled me into a trashcan.

The smell of rotten tomatoes, sour milk, and mildewed chicken blended together made my stomach do flip-flops. A swarm of itchy fruit flies slithered across my arm. I tried to brush them off, but they seemed to reproduce on my skin.

The harder I struggled to get out, the more the kids dragging me howled. One of them thrust my head deeper into the slimy, smelly mess.

Through the grime and stench, I could hear Canfield's voice. "First you don't help me out, next I hear you're talking to the girl I like. You'd better watch your back 'cause we're watching you."

Where were Doc and my teachers? Probably staging a raid in a smoky bathroom. They definitely weren't nearby, so it was no use screaming. Suddenly, I heard a man's voice.

"What's going on here?"

Duke helped me out of the stinky muck, took out his walkie, and called Doc Greely.

He gave Canfield and his buddies a frosty look. "Doc asked me to escort you to his office. It's about time you own up to your actions."

Canfield tossed Duke one of his sarcastic smiles. "You're only a janitor. You can't tell us what to do."

He moved up close in Canfield's face. You couldn't have wedged a sheet of paper between them. "I'm part of this school family, and I care about the people here. I will not allow students to disrespect one another."

Duke started walking toward the office with Kyle, Jason, and Derek shuffling after him.

"I'm watching you, so don't make any wrong moves. Go straight to Doc's office."

"We'll be back, 2K," Canfield mumbled under his breath. Then he and his friends crept along to Doc's office.

"Not if I can help it," Duke said loud enough so they could hear.

Duke walked back to where I was standing, hunched over and dripping with putrid peas and half-eaten Chimichangas. He pointed to the boys' room. "Go clean up. Then meet me in the office."

He was breathing pretty hard now. "You okay, Duke?"

"I've seen better days, but you take what comes your way, and you deal with it." He reached for his inhaler.

"Thanks for what you did," I said.

Duke's soulful brown eyes crinkled into a smile. "Anything I can do to help, you know where to find me."

I could hear him humming "The Duke of Earl" as he made his way to Doc's office.

Everyone in the crowded hallway gaped at me like I was a freak. LeBron looked up from his locker, which was next to the boys' room.

"What happened to you? Looks like you got caught in a food fight."

I shook the garbage off my arms. "No, I haven't been to lunch yet."

LeBron slammed his locker and followed me into the bathroom. "A trash can job then." His voice went up a decibel, and a bunch of guys scurried out of the boys' room.

After they left, he shook his head. "You need to show Kyle and his friends you're a strong person, and you won't take it anymore."

I soaked a paper towel with liquid soap and rubbed my face and arms. "I've tried that."

"Did you try ignoring them?"

"It's hard with the stuff they do." I pulled a clump of greasy noodles from my nose.

He handed me more paper towels. "Come on, let's go to lunch. You'll be okay…" He waved his hand in front of his nose and made a face, "…once you take a shower."

"Thanks, but I have to get to the office."

"Let me know if I can help," he said, hoisting his backpack over his shoulder.

We walked out into the hallway, and a bunch of kids turned around to look at us. I guess they wondered why LeBron would want to be seen with me. After all, he was a star on the football team, and I was wearing Miss Mabel's two-day old tuna noodle casserole.

Along the way to Doc's office, I could see Canfield through the glass partition, waiting in the security office. Where were Jason and Derek?

~ * ~

"Have a seat," Doc said, and I sank into the familiar chair opposite him. "I've informed your father about the incident, and I've given Jason and Derek in-school suspensions. I'm about to call Kyle's parents, so bear with me."

I could see him concentrating on his incident report, making sure he included every gory detail. Doc sounded calm when he dialed the phone, but he drummed his fingers on the desk.

"I have your son here, Mrs. Canfield. I need you and your husband to come to school now."

Through the partition, I could see Kyle making gestures at Doc and mouthing nasty words.

I guess Doc saw him too because he hit the button on his walkie-talkie and told security about Kyle. Officer Grady stormed into the room and gave Kyle a long, hard stare.

Grady yelled so loud I could hear him through the partition. "Calm down, or we'll add threats against a school administrator to your list of offenses."

Kyle mumbled something back, and Grady snapped out at him again before leaving to answer an emergency call from the principal.

Doc left me in his office and went next door to the security office. Kyle had started rummaging through the desk drawer. Doc moved Kyle's hand, slammed the drawer closed and locked it with a key from his chain.

I could hear every word because Doc was talking at top volume.

"What was that, Kyle? On second thought, don't bother. I'm finished listening to you."

Doc called Officer Grady. "Escort Canfield to the principal's office. She already knows the story."

Kyle looked back at me, but I couldn't read the look on his face.

Doc came back in the office and rubbed the sweat off his face with a hand towel he kept in his desk for that purpose. Suddenly, I heard loud knocking. Kyle's parents barged into Doc's office before Doc had a chance to open the door.

"You're picking on our son again, Greely," Kyle's father said.

"Keep this up, and I'll take it straight to the superintendent of schools."

Doc's voice sounded tough, but his hands were shaking. "I'd like you to listen to what happened before you reach any conclusions."

Kyle's father looked like he was about to punch Doc. "Since when do we listen to you? You've done everything you could to mess up Kyle's chance to be a basketball star in high school."

Doc's voice got louder. "There are some things more important than sports."

Mrs. Canfield closed her eyes then opened them. "You mentioned something about Kyle and his friends throwing a student in a trashcan. How do you know our son was the instigator?"

Doc rummaged through a bulging file and then looked up. "Security investigated this and all the other incidents. In every case, Kyle started all of them, and his friends played along."

"That doesn't make them any less guilty," she said.

Doc rubbed the back of his neck. "Naturally, they'll be punished too. We believe once Kyle stops harassing this young man, the others will stop too."

Mr. Canfield pounded his fist on Doc's desk. "How do you know that kid wasn't asking for it? Maybe he did something to bring it on. Kyle and his friends say he's more than a little strange."

I guess Kyle's parents hadn't noticed me sitting off to the side of Doc's office, and frankly, I was glad Doc hadn't bothered to introduce us. I felt like making a run for it, but then they'd know for sure who I was. I buried my head into LeBron's copy of *Catcher in the Rye*.

Dr. Spencer, Holden's history teacher in the story, was telling Holden to get his act together before it was too late. Holden says, "Look, sir, don't worry about me...I'll be all right. I'm just going through a phase right now."

Maybe LeBron was right. I was a lot like Holden, a totally mixed up kid. Like him, I let everything get to me, but who wouldn't in my situation?

Doc turned to Mr. Canfield. "Nobody has the right to abuse other students because of the way they look or act."

Mrs. Canfield made a stop signal with her hand. "Sure, Kyle's had problems like any kid his age, but he's basically a nice kid who made a mistake. You don't want to see the good side of him. He's not the monster you're saying he is."

She turned to her husband, but he looked away. "How about all the times Kyle helped your mom when she was sick? Tell Dr. Greely about that."

His voice was flat. "I don't think that matters now."

She reached into her purse for a tissue and blew her nose. "Doctor Greely, I hope you don't judge Kyle by a few childish pranks. Here's what he's really like. After his grandmother got out of the hospital, he went over and mowed her lawn and sat with her every night while she ate."

Doc lowered his voice. "I hear what you're saying, but that has nothing to do with why we're here today."

Mrs. Canfield was on a roll. "All his teachers gave him good marks in both subject and behavior."

I wanted to shout out, "That's because he has them all conned."

Doc stood his ground like he always does. "You must know it's possible to act one way in front of your teachers and another when you're among peers."

That seemed to shut her up for a while, but Mr. Canfield was another story.

He shook his finger at Doc like it was a weapon. "The school board will hear about this. You'll be mopping floors with that nosy custodian my son told me about."

"Mr. Boardly is a valued member of our staff," Doc said.

"Fine. Then the two of you will enjoy scrubbing toilets together."

Doc threw back his shoulders like he did when he wanted to make himself look taller. "Just so you know, I'd like to settle this in the best way possible. Threats and arguing won't help."

"I agree," Mrs. Canfield said.

Mr. Canfield gave her a look that said "Shut your mouth, woman," and they started out the door. They walked past me like I didn't exist. I guess they had other things on their minds.

Chapter Eight: Watch Your Back

The next day, Dad showed up at Doc's office wearing his charcoal gray suit and navy red- striped tie. Nonna had on her best black dress and the raccoon coat she wore to funerals.

Doc pushed the button on his walkie. "I'd like Duke to be here too."

In a few minutes, Duke barreled into the office in his old jeans and "I'm on island time" t-shirt. He patted me on the shoulder and nodded to Nonna and Dad.

"Duke's a favorite of the students here. He goes out of his way to help Elliot," Doc said.

Nonna shook Duke's hand. "It's good to know somebody cares around here."

Dad took a breath and exhaled.

Nonna started right in on Doc. "You said this wouldn't happen again. I can see you're not a man of your word. I thought you'd do a better job watching those kids."

Dad touched her hand. "Ma, let him explain. I'm sure he's doing his best."

Doc looked at both of them coolly. "Just as you're doing your part to help."

Dad glanced at his pocket watch and shifted in the hard wooden chair. "Sorry to say, I haven't spent much time with Elliot lately. The business is changing. People want bare bones funerals with those plain pine boxes, or worse, cremations. In my dad's day, they marched through the streets of South Philly with a brass band."

Nonna let lose a fake snore, and Doc's eyes widened. Why did she always have to act so goofy?

She bolted out of her seat. "He doesn't need a history of the funeral business from 1940 to the present, Andy."

Doc ignored them and leaned toward me. "We'll do our part by having security keep a closer watch on Canfield and his friends. You have to speak out when they start something, Elliot. Are you willing to do that?"

"Yeah, but they'll probably get back at me worse if I tell on them."

Doc rubbed his cheek. "I don't think you have a choice at this point."

I guess none of us knew what to say, so we sat there staring at one another. It looked like Doc had made up his mind. Did I have the guts to follow through and let him know what they were up to?

Doc turned to Duke. "You've gotten involved in this, Duke, and you've helped other kids. Want to add anything?"

Duke rubbed his stubbly beard. "Doc's right, son. You have to keep us informed. It's not ratting on them. At this point, it's survival. By letting us know what's happening, you may also help someone else who's having a rough time with them. We know they've gone after other kids. Meanwhile, don't roam the halls alone and watch your back."

Funny. That's what Kyle, said.

Nonna glared at him. "Are all of you trying to make my grandson paranoid? Canfield and his friends are the ones doing this. You should be telling them how to act, not my grandson."

"Not to sound rude," Duke said, "but if we want to stop these kids, we have to work together."

Nonna shimmied into her raccoon coat, which made her look like she belonged in a zoo for retired animals. "I have to agree with you there."

Duke shook Dad and Nonna's hands and told Doc he'd keep an eye on things.

Doc reached for Canfield's folder. "For the record, I'm suspending Kyle from school for a week, and Coach has taken him off the court for the rest of the season. He'll also suspend the other two boys from the team for a couple of games."

Doc leaned toward me. "I have to warn you, Elliot. I don't think these boys are finished. It's my guess they're planning a retaliation because they're assuming you're cooperating with us."

Dad and Nonna moved toward the door. "Elliot is smarter than those boys," Dad said. "He can handle this. I have to get to my appointment now. Some folks have scheduled a pre-arrangement conference, and people don't like to be kept waiting, especially when they're planning their own funerals. I'll be in touch."

~ * ~

A couple hours later, I could smell Nonna's roast beef browning in the oven. I knew I couldn't pig out if I wanted to stick to my diet.

Dad came out of his office smiling for a change. "For once, somebody wants an old-fashioned funeral. Rocco Marino said he wants a big send-off, but he can't trust his greedy kids to give it to him. So he's paying fifty thousand dollars for advance arrangements. He wants it to be an extravaganza, like a wedding at the Ritz."

Dad explained how Aida, his assistant, was working out the details.

I almost choked. "You're going to trust Aida with that?"

"Sure," Dad said. "She's a little wifty, but when it comes to talking to people, she knows the right things to say."

Nonna smirked. "Like the time she called the Sullivan's cheapskates because they wouldn't spring for a top of the line casket."

Cousin Aida, Dad's main assistant, came on board when Dad's father ran the business. She did a little bit of everything around the funeral home when she felt like it.

Lately, she used every excuse she could find to get out of work.

She especially loved the funeral directors' convention because she could pig out at the buffets. It runs in the family. Dad said he kept her on to honor his family, so he put up with whatever she did.

Dad looked like he was in a trance and hadn't heard anything Nonna and I said. "Once the people in the neighborhood see Rocco in that spiffy gold hearse, they'll want the same treatment for themselves and their loved ones."

Nonna threw up her hands. "You never hear when people talk, Andy. No wonder Elliot has problems."

Why did they always talk about me like I wasn't here?

Dad smiled. "Save the guilt trip, Ma. Nothing you say can get to me today."

He wrapped his arm around Nonna's scrawny waist. "Things are looking up. Stick that roast in the fridge. We're going out for steak and lobster. Invite Mrs. O'Reilly too."

She tore off her apron and swatted him with it. "Has the embalming fluid you ingest everyday gone to your brain? You're blabbing about a circus funeral and surf and turf while a band of ruffians harasses your poor son. What will they do next, push him off the Ben Franklin bridge?"

"That makes me feel better," I said.

We ended up staying home and eating the roast with Mrs. O'Reilly, who gushed about what a fine young man I was, and how if I lost a little of my baby fat, the girls would worship me like they do her grandson Timmy, who, for the record, weighs ninety-five pounds and has terminal acne.

Dad didn't say two words during dinner. He looked like he was in a trance, probably daydreaming about Mr. Marino's fancy funeral.

Not that Dad was greedy, but like everything else, his business started slacking off when the economy plunged. Naturally, if somebody like Mr. Marino offers to bring him some big bucks, Dad's going to get excited.

What some people don't know is that Dad staged some pretty fancy funerals for people who couldn't afford to pay, and he never asked them for a penny. They wrote an article about him in *the Philadelphia Inquirer*. Nonna had it framed and hung it in the foyer, against Dad's wishes, of course.

Suddenly, my stomach started growling like it always does when I eat puny portions.

When was I going to see results? The scale showed I'd lost only three pounds, and I'd been dieting for a month.

Nonna came out of the kitchen waving her homemade dessert in front of my face. "Warm apple pie with Funky Monkey ice cream."

I looked away, but the yummy scent of fresh apples and cinnamon flew in my nostrils. "Think I'll skip dessert."

Mrs. O'Reilly and Nonna looked at me like I'd grown two noses.

"Duke says losing a little weight might be a good place to start changing my image," I said, heading for the stairs. "Maybe those guys wouldn't annoy me as much."

Nonna trailed me to the stair landing. "The school janitor knows more than your family," she yelled.

"Custodian," I hollered back.

I hurried to my room because I heard my phone ringing. Who else but Roy?

Uncle Pablo said to come in on Saturday for your haircut before he opens for business.

You going to be there?

Wouldn't miss it. I heard Canfield's in big trouble. No more basketball.

Big punishment. What does he have to do before he gets in real trouble? Lock me in a dungeon with a pack of hungry rats?

I heard a couple of Canfield's friends talking. He's spitting mad about being cut out of the games. Says next time he'll do something you won't forget.

Let him. Next time I'm going to fight back.

I would too.

See you Saturday at your uncle's.
Then we'll go to the mall and look for clothes.

~ * ~

Later that night, I could hear Dad and Nonna arguing about how I was starving myself. "That son of yours might become anorexic if he doesn't stop obsessing about calories," Nonna screeched, like she'd forgotten I was in the next room.

"I doubt it, Ma. I've never heard of a boy his size starving to death," Dad said with a chuckle.

As usual, Nonna had the last word. "You think you know everything, Andy, but mark my word, being too skinny is as bad as being too fat."

I didn't let on I'd heard. They didn't know what went on in my head, and I wasn't about to let them in to find out.

I couldn't sleep all night, thinking about my new makeover. I was looking forward to getting out of the rut I was in, but I couldn't stop thinking about what Roy said about what those guys had planned for me.

I tried to act like I could handle it, but I had serious doubts. If things got really rough, would I have the nerve to fight them? If I couldn't handle things myself, would I be able to report them, knowing they might cross the line next time?

Chapter Nine: A New Person

Uncle Pablo was tall and slim like Roy, but deep wrinkles creased his eyes, and he had a bunch of missing teeth.

"*Ay,* what a mop of hair," Uncle Pablo exclaimed when he saw me. "Ready for the new you?"

"Can't wait," I said, "but don't take off too much."

He ran his fingers through my scalp, one layer at a time. Did he think I had head lice?

He looked over his shoulder at Roy, who sat in the swivel chair next to me.

"You want me to give you the athletic look like I gave my nephew?"

Suddenly I panicked. He'd plucked Roy's head clean like a naked chicken.

Roy moved closer to Uncle Pablo. "Elliot wants to look more stylish, but he wants you to leave some hair, at least *un poquito."*

Uncle Pablo nodded. "I understand. When I am finished, you will not recognize yourself."

"That's what I'm afraid of," I said.

"Why are you so nervous? You can trust me. I know what's *muy caliente*, very hot."

He wrapped a plastic cape around my neck and spun me around in the chair so I couldn't see him as he worked. He clipped and cut rapid-fire. I watched my hair fall to the floor in big, curly globs.

Then he buzzed over my scalp with the shaver, around my ears, and under my neck. Did I have any hair left?

"*Mira*," he said, whirling me around so I could see myself. "Is this not a work of art, Roy?"

I'd never heard Roy stutter before.

"It's different. He looks a lot older."

Roy strutted around the barber chair, looking at me from all angles. "Looks like a buzz cut, only shorter, like the guys on my team wear."

He handed me a mirror so I could see the back. I was practically bald.

The words stuck in my mouth. "No offense, Mr. Arroyo, but how long will it take to grow back?"

"Probably three months. Maybe more." His mangy eyebrows formed a question mark. "What? You don't like it?"

I fidgeted in the chair. "It's not what I expected."

"*Muy guapo*. Very handsome. Wait until las chicas at school see you."

"Yeah. I can't wait." Sometimes I could be sarcastic, bordering on mean.

He held out his leathery hand, and I shook it. I had no choice. "From now on, call me Uncle Pablo. We are friends, now, no?"

"No," I said with a vengeance, and he frowned.

Roy ran his hand over my head. "You have to admit, it's a better cut than Mario, the singing barber, gives you."

"Right," I said. I felt like karate chopping him.

I offered Mr. Arroyo a twenty, but he waved my hand away. "You are Roy's friend. It is my pleasure to help you look your best."

Roy and I hopped on the bus and headed for the mall. I wanted to cover my head with one of those bandanas Roy wears.

I touched my bald head again to be sure it had actually happened. "I hope the second half of my makeover goes better than the first."

Roy smacked me on the back and gave me his crazy laugh. "It can't get any worse."

I have to admit, the clothes we picked out made me feel cool. Roy helped me find some basketball shirts and khaki pants. I bought slightly bigger pants because most of the kids wore them on the baggy side, and I didn't want to stand out. A new pair of sneakers completed the outfit. I blew six months of my savings from allowances and gifts, but it was worth it.

~ * ~

Dad was talking on the phone in his room when I got home. He raised his voice, and I listened at the half opened door. Who was he talking to?

"You saw my son at the mall with a baldie haircut? I'm sure he didn't mean anything by it. Of course I think you're a better barber, Mario."

I could hear Mario screaming, and Dad jerked the phone away from his ear.

Dad sighed. "Listen, Mario, they're bringing in Mr. Porcini, the meat cutter at the Italian Market, this afternoon. The family wants his hair done up in one of those wavy pompadours like Liberace's, that dead piano player Ma raves about."

I heard a loud grunt from Mario. When he was mad, he never said much, just grunted and groaned, but Dad and I always knew what he meant. It was like a new language only we could understand.

Dad kept talking non-stop like he always did, hoping Mario would come around. "They want people to remember Porcini as stately and dignified, not with his skimpy hair plastered down like he wore it, with a scuzzy beard that covered his whole face. His wife made it clear how she wants people to remember him. You're the only one who can honor her wishes. I'm depending on you, Mario."

Dad waited for Mario but it looked like he wasn't going to answer until I saw Dad pull the phone away from his ear after Mario shouted at him.

"What? You're quitting?"

Dad dropped the phone and flung his hands in the air. "He hung up..."

"Hope I didn't get you in trouble with Mario," I said.

"Elliot, I didn't see you." I wondered if he ever saw me these days. It seemed like he ate, lived, and breathed dead bodies.

Dad rubbed his temples like he did when he got one of his migraines. "Looks like I'll have to take a crash course in retro hair styles. I don't want to mess up like I did with the Luisis."

Dad was as angry as a Doberman, so I figured now was as good a time as any. I ripped off my hat so he could see my hairless head.

He grimaced. "Why did you have to go to another barber? I would have talked to Mario about giving you the kind of hairstyle you like. Sure, he has a reputation for making people look like they popped out of an old movie, but he also does a mean Mick Jagger and Rod Stewart."

I could feel my voice getting louder. "I don't want to look like Jagger or Stewart. That's why I went to Uncle Pablo."

Dad pointed at my head. "Look where it got you."

He was always saying *I told you so*.

Dad looked like he was going to burst a blood vessel, so I backed down like I usually do. "Want me to talk to Mario?"

"Once he makes up his mind, that's it."

He rubbed his chin and squinted, which he did when he needed inspiration.

He smacked his hands. "Plan B," he said. "I'll get Nonna to help me."

"Don't count on it."

He smiled. "Maybe you can persuade her."

"No chance."

I followed him down the hallway to Nonna's room where she was parked in front of her TV. I hated to be nosey, but I guess it came naturally, living in my house. I wondered how she'd react.

"Ma, I need to talk to you."

"I'm watching my soap opera. Catch me later, Andy."

"Can you help me out, Ma? I need someone to do Mr. Porcini's hair."

Nonna stuck her nose in the air. "The answer to your request is *no*. I've never been good with hair, especially dead people's hair."

"Come on," Dad pleaded. "Just this once."

"A thousand times no. Don't ask again."

Dad stamped his foot like a little kid. Nonna didn't take anything from him, and that got to him.

"What happened to you?" Nonna said, examining my scalp like a brain surgeon. You look like a rap artist from the neck down and a brass knuckle bouncer from Aldo's Bar from the neck up."

"You two don't know what's cool," I said.

~ * ~

The doorbell rang, and I ran downstairs to see who it was.

What was Mom doing here? She had on a white pantsuit with a turquoise flower pinned to the lapel. She looked like she was going to the Academy Awards to stroll the red carpet.

She moved close to me, and her eyes popped out like she was going to hyperventilate.

"What did you do with your gorgeous hair? Why would you want to stand out from the crowd even more?"

I rubbed my hand over my head like a genie might rub a magic lamp.

"I think it actually enhances my appearance." I loved zinging her with sarcasm.

Mom made a face.

"Maybe it will work the other way," I said. "Those kids might think I look so big and bad, they'll fear messing with me."

Mom gave me the same hopeless look Doc does. "Don't count on it."

She took a breath. "I stopped by because I wanted you to know I'm going to the West Coast for a few days to house hunt. I came to say good-bye..."

I felt like I was going to bawl, but I bit my lip so she wouldn't see. "Bye, Mom," I said, hoping she'd think it didn't bother me she was leaving.

Mom stared at me for a long minute. "No hug?"

I gave her a quick hug. I knew she was going away, but I didn't know it would be so soon.

Sometimes, like at this very moment, I felt my friends were more my real family. They never let me down, and I could talk to them about anything.

Dad and Nonna must have heard Mom's voice, so they clomped down the stairs. Dad moved toward her. "Elliot told me your good news about the TV pilot, Rayna. Congratulations. Have a hug for me?"

Nonna closed her eyes and made the sign of the cross.

Mom face brightened. "Sure. Why not, Andrew? We can still be friends even if we can't be married."

They hugged but it wasn't gushy and slobbery like the hugs you see in the movies. It was more like the hug you'd give your great aunt Minnie you haven't seen for a year.

I think in spite of their problems, Dad still loved Mom and she cared about him too, but not enough to move back to the Carnucci Home for funerals and live in the same house with Nonna.

~ * ~

The following afternoon, LeBron and I caught up at the Custard Hut. I wanted Roy to get to know him, so I asked him to meet us there. It's weird how you can be friends with people who are so different.

Roy came out with whatever he was thinking and didn't care if he insulted you if he thought you needed it.

LeBron, on the other hand, liked to analyze everything and kept stuff inside unless he felt strongly about it. Then he'd let it out in one loud scream.

As it turns out, LeBron and Roy had one thing in common, sports. Naturally, they hit it off right away. I liked shooting baskets with them even though I wasn't on the school team and missed more than I dunked. Singing was more my thing.

LeBron cocked his head to get the full impact of my new haircut. "Like your new look, a little short, but so what, hair grows fast."

I looked at Roy somberly. "His uncle did it to me. What can I say?"

Roy let out his famous guffaw. "You never looked so good, amigo. Admit it."

We were about halfway through eating our Atomic, a colossal sundae that served six. Blake Nevins and Tommy Belser, two of Canfield's friends, passed our table, looked back at us, and whispered something.

LeBron gave them a menacing look. "You want to say something, say it to us straight up."

Nevins, the taller one with the Mohawk, leaned over our table, almost toppling my water. "Great haircut."

Belser studied my Sixers shirt. "Didn't know you liked basketball."

I looked him straight in the eye. "You don't know a lot of things about me."

Nevins turned to LeBron, "Why are you hanging out with him? I can understand Arroyo and him being friends..."

Roy jumped out of his chair. "What do you mean by that?"

Nevins smiled. "Just that you two have a lot in common."

"That's true," Roy said, sitting down, "He's my man, and we respect each other."

Roy was quick with comebacks. I wished I could beat those guys at their own game like that.

LeBron's voice boomed so loud the people around us stopped talking. "To answer your question, at least I can have a conversation with him, more than I can say for some people in school."

They shrugged and moved away. LeBron glared at them until they got to the door.

After they left, Roy leaned forward. "Those are the guys I heard talking about what Canfield had planned for you."

"They looked a little nervous to me," LeBron said.

"That's only 'cause you two were here."

Roy let out a loud laugh. "Yeah, 'cause we're so big and bad."

LeBron pointed his finger at me. "That's what you have to do, make them think they can't mess with you. Walk and talk like they can't get to you. That's half the battle."

I had new hair, what little there was, and new clothes. Could I pull off looking like I wasn't a pushover for Kyle and his crew?

~ * ~

When I got to school on Monday, a few kids were hanging around the big wire fence. From a distance, I could see a couple of the Luisi grandchildren in the same ripped up jeans they wore to the funeral.

"Woo hoo, check out the pants," Anna Santiago, one of their friends, said as I walked by. "Watch they don't fall down."

"No chance of that," Elena Luisi said. "His butt's big enough to hold them up."

I gave them a friendly wave and walked in the building. I guess they didn't expect that, and it seemed to work.

I hid my hair with my hat, but as soon as I reached the hall where my locker is, Doc pounced on me. "You know the rules, Elliot. No hats in school."

"Sorry," I said, exposing my naked dome to the entire student body.

Doc scanned me from head to toe and frowned. "Do you honestly think changing your look will help that much?"

"I didn't do it for that reason."

"Why, then?"

"I did it for me."

Doc tugged at his scarecrow brown hair and exhaled slowly.

Derek and Jason, Kyle's friends, made it a point to bump into me when they passed by. "Check out 2K's baldie cut," Jason said. "Wait 'til Kyle sees it."

Derek circled me to catch a better look. "What will Rosalie say?"

I looked him straight in the eye. "Guess we'll have to wait and see," I said, and headed to class.

On Thursday Canfield got reinstated, and he kept his distance from me. Doc reminded me if he came anywhere near me, to tell him right away. It was like those restraining orders you see on TV crime shows. If you get one, you worry things will turn out scarier for you than they were before.

~ * ~

I got to social studies early that day. Rosalie was already there, putting the finishing touches on her term paper about Ralph Bunche, the guy our school's named for. He's famous for being a diplomat and a Nobel Peace Prize winner.

She asked me if I'd proofread her paper. English and math were my best subjects. The topic grabbed my interest right away, so I forgot about the commas and semicolons and concentrated on the message.

Rosalie had put in a quote from Ralph Bunche: "The right to be treated as an equal...is man's birthright. Never permit anyone to treat you otherwise."

Nobody in my family had ever told me stuff like that. I wondered how many people gave that kind of advice to their kids.

After I finished reading, I checked it for grammar.

"No mistakes," I said, handing her back the paper.

"Not even one fragment or misplaced modifier? You know how Mr. Bernstein takes off points for everything."

"It's perfect," I said.

Her face sparkled even without all the makeup the other girls piled on. "You look like you lost a little weight," she said.

I could feel my face flush. "You can see it?"

She had a way of looking at you that made you think she meant everything she said. "I can definitely tell."

I'd lost a few pounds, but no one else noticed, and although my hair didn't fit my face, my clothes made me blend in better with the crowd.

Rosalie smiled. "I have to say, your new haircut took me by surprise."

"In a good or bad way?"

"It doesn't matter what I think. It's how you feel about it that counts."

Even if Rosalie hated it, she'd never deliberately hurt my feelings, or anyone else's for that matter."

"Do you mind if I ask you something?" Right after I'd said it, I felt like taking it back.

She started fiddling with her hair. Was she afraid I was going to ask her out?

"What?" she asked.

"I know it's none of my business, but I wondered if you're going out with Kyle? "

She crinkled her nose like she'd smelled spoiled fish. "Kyle isn't my type. I thought we were friends, but sometimes he takes things too far, like that little trick he pulled with the e-mail he sent you."

I was going to tell her I'd see her around, but instead I surprised myself. "Would you mind if I called or texted you sometime?"

She hesitated. "Okay, and thanks for helping with my paper."

She probably felt sorry for me. But I didn't care. It worked.

I tried to sound cool and confident like Kyle, but my words sounded flat like the guy who takes your cold cut order at the deli counter.

"Sure, no problem," I said.

When class was over, I saw one of Canfield's friends pushing buttons on his cell phone. It looked like it was only a matter of time before

Kyle carried out his threat.

Chapter Ten: Something to Settle

When I got home that afternoon, I could smell Nonna's tomato basil sauce simmering. She was making lasagna, my favorite dish, with layers of luscious pasta, ground beef, hot sausage, and ricotta cheese, smothered in her chunky tomato gravy and topped with Romano cheese.

"Your dad's waiting for a body from the hospital. Wicked accident on I-95. Thirty-five-year-old man dozed off at the wheel."

Once Nonna got started, she didn't stop.

"If that's not bad enough, he has Mr. Porcini's hairdo to worry about."

Nonna sandwiched the meat mixture between the noodles, sauce, and mozzarella. She pointed to the heavy lasagna pan, and I shoved her masterpiece in the oven.

I broke off a small piece of Italian bread and ate it without butter. "Maybe Roy's Uncle Pablo can help Dad with the hair."

Nonna chuckled. "Get real. The Porcinis don't want his head to look like a naked baby's butt."

"Dad might like the idea. He needs the help, and lately he hates touching the bodies."

Nonna knit her brows. "He's never been squeamish about the bodies before. Maybe the idea of his own mortality is starting to creep up on him."

"I don't know," I said, sneaking another hunk of bread, "I think he gives too much to the job and it's doing him in."

Nonna gave me one of her crushing hugs. "Your dad's going to be fine. I'll make sure of it. That goes for you too. My mission in life is to see that my two men come out on top."

I broke away from her grip and set out the plates and silverware.

She wiped her hands on her red, white and blue apron that said "Women Belong in the House and in the Senate."

It almost killed me to put my fork down at dinner. No wonder Nonna's lasagna had won a gold medal at the South Philly Food Festival.

I was starting to think about why I'd lost only a few pounds when I'd cut back so much. Maybe I had a tumor growing in my stomach like one of Dad's customers. When you live with dead people, you start getting paranoid about dying from their illnesses.

She inspected my plate. "What's wrong? You sick or something?"

"No, it tasted great, but I have a ton of school work."

I helped her clear away the dishes and stack the dishwasher, and she spooned the leftovers into plastic containers for Dad. Then she was off to play bridge with Mrs. O'Reilly and her friends at the senior center.

At last, I was alone in the house except for Mr. Porcini. He was up on the third floor, waiting for Dad to transform him into Liberace.

Suddenly, I had the urge to call Rosalie. Somehow that seemed more personal than texting her. To my surprise, she answered right away. I figured she'd be busy with her friends, but I heard she only had a couple of close friends like I did. She didn't belong to any one crowd.

The word around school was that a couple of popular girls were madly in love with Canfield, so I'm sure they were thrilled to hear she didn't like him.

Hi, it's me, Elliot.

Hi. I can only talk for a minute. I'm going to drama rehearsal.

Was she making an excuse? Roy said I had to stop thinking that way.

Maybe you should think about trying out for the school musical. We're doing "Man of La Mancha."

Thanks, but I don't know if I'm good enough to get a part. I heard a lot of kids try out.

I caught your solo in chorus. You sounded awesome. And they need male singers. Mr. Diggs, the drama coach, couldn't find enough boys to play in 'South Pacific." He had to go to Coolidge High to recruit them.

I'll think about it. I'm taking singing lessons, and I really like them.

Okay, don't forget to sign up. Mom's calling me for dinner. Talk to you later.

When I got downstairs, Dad was sprawled out on Nonna's favorite red silk sofa pigging out on lasagna and salad with Nonna's house dressing with those stinky Gorgonzola sprinkles.

His mouth was full, and I could hardly make out what he was saying.

"How are things at school?"

"Nothing I can't handle."

He broke off a chunk of Italian bread from a big loaf and slathered it with a fist-sized chunk of butter.

"If those kids start anything, let that vice principal know right away."

I nodded, but I'd already decided telling Doc would make things worse. They'd find out, and I'd be dead meat.

I sat down next to him, and he swung his legs out of the way to give me room.

"Can we talk for a minute?"

"Don't have a whole lot of time now, son. Have two bodies to restore. Maizie's off today, so I'm on my own with the make-up. Aida's at a catering seminar to look into a new line of work. I can't wait for the day she retires. The down side is I have to do the embalming, the hair, *and* the make-up myself. I was planning on winding up early so I could watch that Sixers-Pistons game."

He took a swig of his root beer and looked at me. "Can we talk later?"

"It will only take a minute. I heard about your problem finding someone to do hair, and I was thinking..."

Dad looked at me slyly. "Are you offering to help?"

"Not really, but I have an idea. I was thinking Uncle Pablo could help you, at least with the hair. He's got a lot of experience."

Dad struggled out of the sofa, leaving his dishes on the coffee table. "Thanks, but I'd go out of business if he touched my clients. Families like the bushy, full look, not the sparse, scalped look."

He gave me his end-of-conversation look. "Have to get back to work. I'll catch up with you as soon as I can. Keep me up on how things are going, okay?"

~ * ~

A couple days later, the three of us met Doc for a family conference before school.

Dad looked up at the clock on Doc's wall and shifted in his chair. "I have two funerals back to back, so we can't stay long."

Nonna leaned over Doc's desk. "We want to put an end to this today."

"Very well, Mrs. Carnucci," Doc said, "but we need to remain calm if we want to help Elliot."

Nonna stood up, but next to Doc she looked like one of the seven dwarves. "Don't talk down to me, young man."

"Relax, Ma," Dad said. "He's trying to help."

Nonna gave Dad a fierce look before settling into one of Doc's dilapidated chairs.

"Where's Duke?" I asked. "He said he'd be here."

"He couldn't make it," Doc said. "He came down with bronchitis this weekend. Been getting it a lot lately. He left this note for you."

He handed me a sealed envelope with my name on it. I stuffed it in my backpack.

Doc leaned back in his chair and studied me like he was a shrink and I was his patient. "So, Elliot. Do you think the trouble has subsided somewhat since the trash can incident?"

Why couldn't he talk like a normal person?

"Somewhat," I said, mimicking him.

Nonna elbowed me. "Give him a straight answer. Are those thugs still pestering you or not?"

"Easy, Ma," Dad said. "He's not finished talking."

"Actually, I was. The fact is I'm wondering if they're ever going to stop."

"Why do you say that?" Doc asked.

I looked straight into Doc's sleepy eyes. "If you were overweight, got straight A's, and lived in a funeral home, do you think you'd be voted the most popular kid in the class?"

Dad's face reddened. "Elliot…"

Doc stared out the window. "I think I can relate to what you're saying. I had my share of ribbing when I was a boy. A couple of kids used to call me *Fat Boy* and *Brainiac*. Even worse, they tripped me and put dog excrement in my locker. When I got to high school, I finally learned how to deal with it."

Did he know kids still made fun of him?

"What did you do to make it stop?" I asked.

"My friend encouraged me to go to my school counselor. At first, I didn't want to because I was afraid they'd get back at me, but then I decided I had to do something if I wanted those kids to stop. I asked the counselor not to tell them I'd said anything, and she kept her word. As it happened, she called the kids in along with their parents, and they promised to stop when their parents said they'd get punished. Things weren't perfect for a while, but eventually the bullying stopped.

"Lucky you," I said.

Nonna boxed my arm. "Don't be a wise guy."

"Of course it's a different ball game now," Doc said. "You've got drugs, weapons, broken homes…"

Dad and Nonna exchanged looks.

Doc let out a nervous cough. "Naturally, I didn't mean in your case, Mr. Carnucci. I can see you're doing your best to give Elliot a decent upbringing."

It was too late. Dad stood up and straightened his tie. "I don't think this is going anywhere."

Nonna shook her finger at Doc. "If anything else happens to my grandson, I'm going to hold you responsible."

I could see a vein pulsing in Dad's head. "Ma, you're not helping matters. Let's see what Elliot has to say."

They all looked at me like I was the Oracle of Delphi.

"In case you haven't noticed, I'm losing weight. I have a couple of friends."

Doc nodded. "That's a good start..."

Nonna scowled at Doc. "You have a habit of patronizing people, and I don't like it. My grandson's doing everything he can."

Nonna loved using big words to put people in their place, but Doc knew every word in the dictionary.

Dad stood up and smoothed his rumpled pinstriped suit. "We need to go now. Call me if there's a problem."

Nonna planted a big, slobbery kiss on my forehead. I tried to back away, but it was too late. I wiped off her coral lipstick with the back of my hand.

"I don't want to hear there's a problem," she said to Doc. "It's up to you to stay on top of the situation. That's why we pay you administrators big bucks."

I could see Doc clenching his fists under the table. He got up and shook Dad's and Nonna's hands. "I'll do my best."

~ * ~

By the time Doc sent me back to homeroom, Ms. Begley had finished taking roll. She looked at my note from Doc and whited-out the absence in her book.

When she turned her back to write on the board, Kyle blew up his cheeks and widened his hands. That was his way of calling me two tons without using words. I don't know what came over me, but I made a *W* for *whatever* with my hand. A few kids laughed. Were they on my side or making fun of me? Who could tell?

Ms. Begley heard them and turned around.

"That's enough," she said, and everyone got back to doing homework they hadn't finished the night before.

"I wouldn't do that if I were you, 2K," Kyle whispered. "By the way, see you at lunch. We have something to settle."

Was Kyle threatening me, or was he just trying to scare me? I wondered if I should tell Doc what he'd said. Things were getting pretty heavy.

One thing I knew for sure. I didn't need the name *rat* added to the other names those guys called me.

Chapter Eleven: The Rats That Ate New York

Everything was quiet until March the 15th, The Ides of March. That's what Shakespeare called it in Julius Caesar, a play we read in honors English. That was the day Caesar's friend Brutus killed him. I felt a little nervous thinking about it.

Could thinking about something like that make a person more open to bad stuff happening? Nonna thought so. She also believed if a black cat crossed your path you were doomed forever.

I headed for the lunchroom, hoping I wouldn't meet up with Canfield and his friends. Every so often, I turned around to check things out.

I remembered Roy was skipping lunch for track practice. He had a major meet coming up. LeBron looked up from his book and signaled to me from across the room.

Miss Mabel handed me my tuna platter because I wasn't polishing off burgers and fries these days. I felt someone tugging at my collar.

I turned around, and who was directly in my face, but Kyle. His handsome features and bright strip-whitened teeth didn't make up for his flushed face and stale tobacco breath.

"Stay away from Rosalie." He spat out each word, and his saliva flew in my face.

"We're just friends."

I moved away, but he reached for my collar.

"Hey, let go. You're strangling me."

Miss Mabel smacked her hands on her hips. "Let him go, or I'll call Officer Grady."

Canfield chuckled. "You don't have to do that. We're just messing around. Aren't we, 2K?"

"Yeah, nothing I can't handle." I hid my hands behind my back because they were shaking like crazy.

Miss Mabel crossed her arms and looked at the cafeteria lady next to her. "Maybe you can give this boy his lunch, Gladys," she said, pointing to Canfield. "I'm not waiting on him today."

Kyle cocked his head at Miss Mabel. "You can get fired for that. My neighbor's on the school board."

She waved her spatula at him. "Not if I told what you did, you little hellion. Now scat."

Canfield followed me to my table. "Tell Rosalie you won't be able to talk to her anymore."

"How did you know that?"

Had he planted spies in my house?

"I have my ways." He looked at me like I was the doofus of the century. "One of Rosalie's friends told me you called her."

LeBron was sitting at the table reading *Native Son*. I sat down across from him.

He looked up at Canfield. "You wanted to see me about something?"

Canfield backed away. "I was just leaving."

"Good. 'Cause I don't like being interrupted when I'm reading, except maybe by my friend here."

Canfield moved closer. "I'm talking to you, Carnucci."

"I'm busy now. I don't have time to talk."

Did I actually say that? I could hear the words, but my voice seemed like it was coming from somebody else.

LeBron gave him a menacing look. "You heard him."

Canfield cursed under his breath. He picked up the pace to catch up with Jason and Derek at the other end of the lunchroom.

Miss Mabel had her cell phone pressed to her ear. I hoped she wasn't calling Doc. Telling on Kyle would be my death knell, considering how riled up he was.

"Thanks," I said to LeBron.

He stuffed his book in his backpack. "Wouldn't matter if I was here or not. You handled him right. Keep standing up to him, and he'll get the message."

Suddenly, I remembered the letter Doc gave me. I poked around in my backpack and unfolded it. "From Duke. Want to hear it?"

"If you want me to," LeBron said.

I read it quietly so only LeBron would hear.

Elliot:

Sorry I missed the meeting at school, but I've been thinking about you. You asked me if I had any ideas about dealing with those guys. It so happens I do. I think they might help, but it's up to you which ones you want to try.

One thing you might want to do is get involved in a new activity. I know you're in Mathletes, but it might help to try something different types of kids get involved in, not just the brainy kids. If other kids get to know you better, they won't be so quick to judge or make fun of you like Kyle and his friends do.

Another thing you might want to think about. There's always somebody who's going through what you're going through. At least that's what Mother told me when I was coming up. Maybe reaching out to these kids who have problems like yours might help you. You just have to find a way to do it.

Eventually those boys will get tired of picking on you when they see there's no payoff. There will be an end to the bad days. Things will get better.

See you in school.

William Walker Broadly, AKA, Duke

I looked out the open lunchroom window, and I could see the sun peeking through. I was starting to feel warm, so I took off the Sixers basketball jacket I always wore to the lunchroom. Could winter be over for good?

LeBron stopped chomping on his cheeseburger and looked up at me. "I hear Duke's not doing well."

"Doc says he has bronchitis, and I hear him wheezing a lot."

"Not what I meant."

A swarm of birds started chirping and almost drowned out LeBron's voice. I leaned forward to hear him.

My heart began to pound. "What then?"

"My grandma knows him from church. She says they're testing him for lung cancer."

I pushed my tuna salad around the plate with my plastic fork. Suddenly I didn't feel hungry.

"He doesn't even smoke."

LeBron chug-a-lugged his chocolate milk. "The people he works with do, but that's not the worst of it."

"What do you mean?"

“He's had a heart condition, atrial fibrillation, for a few years. Sometimes he gets bouts of rapid heartbeat that land him in the hospital. That could mean big trouble on top of his lung problem."

"Does he have family or anyone else who can help him?"

"Grandma says he's all alone. Lost his wife a long time ago. She says his two daughters don't spend much time with him. They both have important jobs with the government."

"Any grandkids?"

LeBron ripped open a pack of cream-filled cupcakes. "No. Guess his kids are too busy to have babies."

I put my half-finished lunch on the tray. "How can he work if he's that sick?"

"Probably wants to keep his mind off it. Grandma says he's a fighter."

The bell rang, and everyone raced out of the lunchroom.

I told LeBron I'd catch him later. I fell into the mechanical rhythm of kids racing to class, shouting, laughing, slamming lockers, but somehow I felt apart from everything–cut off and alone. Duke had a serious illness, and there was nothing I could do about it.

~ * ~

Later that day, we had to give a speech in language arts. Just thinking about it made me sweat, which always seemed to turn into body odor.

Ms. Williams said she wanted us to talk about a big change in our lives and how it affected us. She'd also asked us to hand in a copy of the speech with no grammar or spelling mistakes. You could use a brief outline, but nothing more. She said to talk like we'd talk to a friend.

How could I do that with Canfield sitting there ready to pounce on me if I made a mistake?

Ms. Williams clutched her black vinyl grade book. Her rimless glasses fell down on her nose, making her look like Torquemada, the maniac judge from the Spanish Inquisition we'd learned about in social studies.

"Volunteers first," she said. "Remember, this is a major writing/speaking exam, so it can make or break you."

Ms. Williams was big on alternative assessment exams like that because there was no way you could cheat like you could on a multiple choice or true and false test.

More than anything, I wanted to get it over with. My hand shot up, a reflex action. Then I put it down, but I knew it was too late because I saw her looking my way.

"Elliot, thanks for volunteering. We'll start with you."

Kyle and one of his friends rolled their eyes.

Ms. Williams moved from behind her desk and stood in front of the class with her arms folded. "I'll also grade each of you on audience participation. That means no calling out, wisecracks, or gestures."

Why did she say that? Was it because she knew how some kids bugged me, or was it a general comment meant for everybody? My greatest wish was to be anonymous like I was before Kyle came on the scene. Would that ever be possible?

I stumbled up to the front of the room. I took off my glasses, which was a bad idea, because I was almost totally blind without them.

Ms. Williams turned her back to answer the phone, and Canfield whispered *2K*, just loud enough for me to hear.

She turned back to the class, but too late to catch Canfield. "Principal Ríos will ring the bell a few minutes early this period so you can get a head start on the weekend."

A loud cheer rang out, and everybody started packing up.

She flicked the lights off and on, and the class quieted down. She was big on after school detentions and calling homes, so no one messed with her.

"Elliot, we'll have just enough time for your speech. We'll hear the others next week."

I cleared my throat and leaned on my right foot, then my left. By some miracle, the class quieted down.

Oh, no. I'd had grabbed my math homework instead of my speech outline.

Ms. Williams looked at me. "What is it?"

"Can I go back to my desk? I seem to have..."

She looked up at the clock. "We're on a tight schedule. You'll need to start now."

There was no way I was going to get out of it.

Kyle put his hand over his mouth and whispered something to the girl beside him, and they both laughed.

LeBron frowned at them, and they looked away.

Suddenly, everyone got quiet.

"My speech is called 'My Happiest Moment: My Parents' Divorce.'"

I forgot about my notes and started talking like I would to Roy or LeBron.

"Most kids think divorce is the end of the world. They're shuffled from parent to parent. They won't be able to see their friends as much because they're always moving from one house to another. They might even have to change schools.

"In my case, it's the opposite. I'm glad my parents broke up. They don't scream and call one another names anymore. In fact, they get along better than they did before.

"I live with my dad, who's so busy with his business he doesn't have time to check up on me. My grandmother lives with us, and she makes up for it. She's like a PI and the FBI rolled into one. She knows what I'm going to do before I know. When Mom and Dad were together, she was always butting in their business, which was one of the reasons Mom left.

"In the end, my parents decided they were better apart than together, and they've been that way ever since. Of course, I miss Mom 'cause she moved to the west coast to make a TV pilot. When I see her, it's like we're on vacation. We all get along better than when we lived together."

I paused like I was a newscaster on TV. "Divorce was the best thing for our family, but every family has to decide for themselves."

Ms. Williams smiled. "Thanks, Elliot. I got a lot out of your story. Your speech proves it's not so much what happens to you, but how you look at things."

I heard a few feeble claps from scattered sections of the room. Then the bell rang and it was time to leave.

LeBron gave me a thumbs up.

When we got into the hall, I cornered LeBron, "What made me tell them all that? Now everyone knows my life story."

"That might be a good thing. Maybe they'll see you in a different way."

I was anxious to leave the building and forget about my speech.

"Want to shoot baskets with me and Roy this weekend?" LeBron asked on the way to my locker.

"Sounds good. Call me," I said, spinning three – ten – eleven to open my lock.

From the top shelf of my locker came a high-pitched squealing. My face must have turned the color of one of Dad's dead bodies because LeBron grabbed my shoulder to prop me up.

LeBron lifted the cardboard box where the noise came from, and we looked in. Two super-sized gray rats peered out and bared their incisors at us.

I covered the box with my gym towel and belted out the backdoor to the dumpster. LeBron followed me.

"Wait. Let's show this to Doc. He should know what those guys are up to."

"No," I said, overturning the box and watching the huge rodents run toward the garbage smell. "They did this because they think I told on them."

~ * ~

When I got home, I called Duke. Luckily, he'd given me his number and said to call him if I needed to talk.

"Guess who this is?" I asked.

"Spiderman? The Phantom of the Opera or could it be my friend Elliot?

"How are you feeling?" I asked.

"Fair to middling," he said and chuckled. He loved to laugh at his own silly sayings.

"Thanks for the note."

He took deep breaths between words, and it was a little hard to understand him. "Wanted you to know I was thinking about you. How's it going? Any new developments?"

"Not really," I said.

He started coughing, and I thought he'd never stop. "Come on, son. You can't fool The Duke."

"Why do you say that?"

"It's not what you say so much as your tone."

Should I tell? He was bound to find out anyway.

"They left a souvenir in my locker," I said.

"A sign like the one in the boys' room?"

"Nope. The Rats That Ate New York, big rats like the ones in 'The Pied Piper.'"

His voice sounded scratchy. "What are you going to do?"

"What would you do?"

"I'm no snitch, but in this case, I'd tell Doc. That's big time harassment."

Why did I call him if I knew what he was going to say?

"I'll think about it."

His voice sounded like it did when he blasted out kids in homeroom for sticking gum under their desks. "That means you won't."

"Probably not."

After I hung up, I found this text from Rosalie:

We can't talk anymore.

Call me. Will explain.

Chapter Twelve: The Poufy Pompadour

I could see our parking lot from my window. By six thirty, people were starting to pull in for the Porcini viewing, oversized Cadillacs and Lincolns filled with aunts and uncles leaning on canes, walkers, or one another. Children and grandchildren poured out of SUVs and moved toward the front door.

Nonna poked her head in my room. "What's up with you, big shot? Too busy to talk to Nonna? I saved you fried chicken and mashed potatoes from lunch. Figured your Dad and I would eat early because of the funeral."

"Thanks, but I bought burgers and fries on the way home."

I hated lying but she'd make a scene about my having an eating disorder if she knew I'd eaten carrot sticks and yogurt. The mourners would hear, and Dad would give me a guilt trip for disrespecting Mr. Porcini and his family.

Nonna craned her neck to see out my window. "Looks like a record crowd and I know why. That Porcini knew how to carve a rump roast so it would taste like filet mignon. His leg of lamb made your mouth water."

I rolled my eyes. "How did the hair go? Did you talk to Dad?"

She snickered. "It took him hours, but he finally got it right. He plugged in those jumbo hot rollers your mother left behind. Don't tell, or she'll never use them again. He also found some molding wax in your bathroom. Mr. Porcini's a dead ringer, excuse the pun, for Liberace with that poufy pompadour. Want to take a peek?"

Nonna was afraid of death but she was also fascinated by it, so she had to see all the bodies. I don't think anybody minded because she always gave the closest relative one of her homemade rosaries and told them she'd pray for the repose of the deceased's soul, and she did. Whenever someone died, she'd light up her room like a bonfire with a zillion of those votive candles you pay a dollar each for in church.

I followed Nonna down the winding, circular staircase to the reposing room. The sharp smell of carnations and the sweetness of gardenias made me dizzy. I could hear old Elvis crooning "Love Me Tender" on the sound system.

Dad always asked people what kind of music the dead person liked and went out of his way to find it. Mr. Porcini collected Elvis memorabilia and displayed it in his butcher shop. He even visited Graceland once, and he and his wife had a picture taken with Elvis' wife, Priscilla.

Some said the dead people's relatives liked Beethoven, Bach, or Bruce Springsteen. One family played "You Are the Sunshine of My Life" by Stevie Wonder, and another brought in their own rap group.

I was relieved Dad didn't decide to play "You Ain't Nothin' But a Hound Dog" like Nonna suggested. She reminded us how Mr. Porcini played it when he hacked away at the bloody cow carcasses hanging from hooks in his butcher shop. Thinking of it made me never want to eat hamburger again.

We crept into the room. The whole family knew me from the neighborhood, so it didn't look like I was gawking or anything.

I shook some of the dead people's relatives' hands and told them I was sorry about their loss and I'd always remember how Mr. Porcini bowled a perfect game in Dad's league. Nonna squeezed my hand like she was going to break it as we filed past the casket.

I took a quick look. Nonna was right. Everything was perfect from the pompadour hairstyle to his wing-tipped shoes. To make things even better for Dad, some of the same people from the Luisi funeral, like Viola; the widow, and Carmine, her sumo wrestler brother, showed up to pay their respects to the Porcinis.

I thought Mr. Porcini's *presentation*, the term Dad used for how the bodies looked, would more than make up for the bad dye job he'd given Mr. Luisi.

In clear ear shot of the Luisis, the Porcinis told Dad he was a genius, and Mama Porcini invited our whole family over for a chicken cacciatore dinner with homemade cannolis, after a respectable period of mourning, of course.

I wasn't going to hold my breath for that invitation because that day would probably never come. Everyone knew she and Mr. Porcini were still madly in love after seventy years and that she'd probably wear black and suffer from terminal depression until the day she died

One of the pictures she gave Dad to display on an easel next to the casket showed the Porcinis looking into each other's eyes like they couldn't live without one another, sort of like I picture things when I daydream about Rosalie. I don't remember Mom and Dad ever looking at one other that way.

After I shook all the Porcinis' hands a zillion times and told them how I'd miss going to the Phillies games and eating hot dogs with Mr. Porcini, I dragged myself up to my room.

~ * ~

I was about to call Rosalie when Nonna barged in and began picking my brain for crossword puzzle answers.

"What's wrong? You're not as swift as you usually are. Something happen at school?"

"No, but I'm busy. Have to finish my homework."

"It's the weekend. You have 'til Monday."

"No offense, Nonna, but I need some time alone."

"Well!" She said, and stormed out.

The whole time I was at the service, I thought about Rosalie's text. Why did she say she couldn't talk to me? Was she having second thoughts about our friendship?

My fingers itched to speed dial Rosalie's number. I felt relieved when she answered on the third ring.

"It's Elliot."

She paused. "Let me check to see if anyone's listening."

I didn't hear anything but her radio tuned to the cool jazz station. "It's okay. My parents are downstairs watching TV."

I got right to the point. "So why can't we talk?"

"Kyle threatened to beat you up if I had anything to do with you. He whispered it to me in math."

I didn't have to think about it. Giving in would only make it worse. "I say we shouldn't listen to him. He'll do what he wants whether we talk to each other or not."

She took her time answering. "I don't know."

"It's up to you. I don't want to pressure you."

I guess she didn't know what to say because she got totally quiet.

"Let me know what you decide one way or the other," I said.

"You're right," she finally said. "We shouldn't let him stop us from talking. Kyle bosses too many people around, and he always wins."

"I'm glad you decided that. Once we start playing by his rules, he'll think he can do anything he wants to anybody."

"Somebody needs to stand up to him," she said.

Was I strong enough to follow thorough? I'd gotten a taste of what he and his friends could do, and it wasn't fun.

"Elliot, you still there?"

"I was thinking, when is that audition for the school show?"

"It's coming up soon. Want me to tell Mr. Diggs you're interested?"

"Why not?" I said. "See you in social studies."

I sat at my desk trying to sort things out. Duke might be very sick, I'd just heard Canfield wanted to beat me up, and I'd decided to ignore his threats. I should have felt lousy, but I didn't. It was weird, but I actually felt hopeful, like maybe things weren't as bad as they seemed.

Chapter Thirteen: A Younger Version of Dad

A week later, Dad called to me from the kitchen as I started out the door. "Have a minute?"

If I left now, I'd barely make the I-Max rainforest show at the Franklin Institute, where I was meeting Roy and LeBron. It was also raining hurricane speed, so I'd have to wait twice as long for the bus. "Okay, but I'm going out with my friends, and I don't want to keep them waiting..."

Dad had on his striped pjs and was chomping on a cinnamon raisin bagel slathered with cream cheese. "Here's the deal. I expect a huge crowd tonight for Julio Santiago, the man who got killed on I-95. I'm short-handed in the meet and greet department."

"Anything I can do to help?"

Dad washed his bagel down with black coffee. "I was thinking you could welcome people and take their raincoats and umbrellas."

Dad had never let me help at services before. I felt excited and nervous at the same time, but what if Kyle and his friends heard about it? It would give them one more thing to bug me about. I could hear them saying *Elliot the ghoul, Elliot the body snatcher.*

I searched the closet for my umbrella, but all I could find was Nonna's oversized red one with yellow smiley faces plastered all over it.

"Naturally, I'll pay you," he said.

Getting paid to talk to people sounded like a good deal. Better than my paper route where I had to peddle around the neighborhood at five AM and dodge people's vicious dogs. "I could use the extra cash."

Dad looked at me, and then suddenly stared out the window like he does when he's remembering something he doesn't want to. "At least you have a choice. As soon as I got my drivers' license, my dad made me drive the dead wagon and pick up bodies. I had to help hoist them on to the embalming table. He forced me to watch as he drained blood from the bodies and pumped in embalming fluid. He told me my pay was gaining experience for my future as a third generation funeral director."

"I guess there are some advantages to being your son," I said.

Dad cut himself a piece of Nonna's buttery crumb cake. "Are you saying you appreciate me?"

He put his hand on my shoulder. I knew how hard it was for him to get close and to show affection, even to me. That was one of the things Mom complained about before she left. Could it be that because of his job he was super aware of what it would be like to get close to someone and then lose them?

Most of his customers said he was a great comfort to them and one of the warmest men they'd ever met. Were they talking about my dad?

I guess you don't have to risk much when you're dealing with people outside your family, so it's easier to be who you really are with people who aren't related. Maybe that's why I feel so comfortable when I'm around Roy and LeBron.

Dad walked me to the door. "Have fun with your friends."

"Thanks for giving me the chance to help." I was so happy I almost floated out of the house.

~ * ~

After the 3D show, I told Roy and LeBron about my first official job as a funeral director's assistant.

"Cool," Roy said. "If your dad has any more openings, I've got a black suit. I could stuff an ascot in my pocket."

LeBron's eyes lit up. "I wouldn't mind helping. I could be the bouncer if anybody starts a fight like you said they did at that Luisi funeral. I want to teach high school, so it would be good practice being a referee."

"I'll tell Dad. Maybe he can use you guys if the hairdresser or nail person doesn't show."

LeBron hesitated. "I'll think about it."

Roy shuddered. "Same for me, amigo."

Why were people, even fearless guys like Roy and LeBron, put off by talking about something as natural as death?

I couldn't resist razzing them. "Did I ever tell you how peoples' fingernails and hair grow after they die?"

Roy and LeBron looked at each other.

"We don't want to know," Roy said.

I couldn't wait to see the expressions on their faces when I told them. "That's one of those weird things everyone wonders about. It's actually an optical illusion. People dehydrate after they die. The flesh dries, and it pulls away from the nails and hair. It makes it look like the nails and hair keep growing."

Roy made a face. "How do you know that stuff?"

I smiled. "One of the benefits of living in a funeral home."

"Here's something I've always wondered about," LeBron said.

"Just ask," I said. I was beginning to feel like I knew stuff nobody else did, and it felt good.

LeBron was starting to get into it. "I've heard dead bodies sometimes make noises like they're still alive. How do you explain that?"

Roy scrunched up his nose. "Come on, guys. You're making me want to barf, and my parents are taking me out for Indian food."

I waved him away and looked at LeBron. "Yeah, a body can make an almost human sound, something between a sigh and a groan. Sometimes when we move the bodies, air flow escapes past the vocal cords. This can cause the body to make strange sounds. One of Dad's helpers got so freaked out, he ended up quitting."

LeBron shuddered. "That's why I'm going to be a teacher."

"That's why I'm never coming to your house again," Roy said, and almost burst my eardrums with his crazy laugh.

Roy's eyes looked wild. "Picture this. Wouldn't it be fun to trap Canfield and a couple of his friends in the room where they prepare the bodies? Make it so they couldn't get out?"

LeBron rubbed his hands. "Yeah, Kyle and his boys would bang on the door and scream like you did when they locked you in the supply closet. Meanwhile, the bodies keep making groaning noises and maybe sitting up like I heard they do sometimes."

"Great idea," I said, "but Nonna and Dad would catch us before we could pull it off. Or I'd say, 'Sure, go for it.'"

~ * ~

By the time I got home, Nonna was in the kitchen dishing out shrimp fried rice from cardboard containers.

"No time to cook. Mrs. O'Reilly and I are going on a double date with Armand, the plumber, and his brother Joey."

I dropped my diet soda can, and it spilled all over the glass table. "You're going on a date?"

Nonna handed me a roll of paper towels. "Why? Didn't think I could get one?"

Before I could answer, we heard a few loud honks from a car horn outside.

Dad leaped from his chair. "What's all that noise?"

Nonna moved the curtains so she could peek out the window. "It's those two old rascals, Armand and Joey Cacciatucci, honking the horn. Catch Peg O'Reilly sitting in the backseat like she's the Queen of England."

She came back to the table. "They can sit there and honk all night for all I care. I'm not going out with a man who doesn't know enough to come to the door for a lady."

Dad rubbed the back of his neck. "The Santiago's will arrive for the visitation in one hour. We can't have this racket outside."

Nonna peered in her compact mirror and slicked on fiery red lipstick. "Let him in, Elliot, and don't act like you're shocked I'm going on a date."

Armand, the plumber, trailed by his brother Joey, followed me into our private entrance. Nonna's date reminded me of a gorilla with his slick black hair. A handlebar mustache hung over his blubbery lips like a squirrel's tail. He smelled like he'd fallen into a vat of expensive aftershave, which threw Dad into a choking fit.

His brother Joey, who was decked out in a three-piece suit, nodded and smiled but didn't say a word. Maybe he was what they called socially challenged, or in simple terms, shy.

Armand grabbed Nonna's hand and tried to kiss it, but she pulled it back like it was a rattlesnake.

"My apologies, Angela," he said in a hushed voice. "I didn't mean to offend you. Your friend Peg told us to wait outside because it might disturb your son's business."

"Likewise for me," Joey echoed him and took a little bow.

"His customers are dead," Nonna said. "You disturbed *me* because you didn't come to the door."

I could sense Dad wanted them to leave. He needed time to organize his thoughts before the funeral. He always made it a point to call all the family members by name. What he loved most was standing around in his pinstriped suit, arranging gladioli and carnations, and shaking hands like he's running for president.

I put on my navy blue suit, a white shirt and a blue and gold tie. Pablo's hairstyle was starting to grow out, so I slicked it back with the molding wax Dad used on Mr. Porcini's pompadour. That would have totally grossed Mom out.

I slipped into Dad's bedroom and stared at myself in the full-length mirror he looked in before he faced the families. My pants hung on me 'cause I'd finally lost some weight, but otherwise, I looked like a younger version of Dad.

My legs felt rubbery and my hands got clammy thinking about my first day of work for Dad. Would I know what to say and not goof up and embarrass Dad?

~ * ~

I was surprised to find out that once I got to the reposing room, I felt like I did when I had to sing a solo, calm and relaxed, like I knew what to do all along.

The first thing I noticed was that Dad gave Mr. Santiago a closed coffin and put his picture on top of it. Dad told the family he was burned beyond recognition, and it would be impossible to make him look like they remembered him.

He suggested the family create a collage with pictures from important moments in his life. Dad put them near the guest book on the fancy oak table in the lobby so people might think of him the way he had looked when he was alive.

When I saw Anna Santiago, one of his four kids, kneeling in front of the casket, I made the connection right away.

Woo hoo, check out the pants. She was the girl in the schoolyard laughing about my new look. I'd never actually talked to her, but she was in my gym class.

She looked like she was going to pass out as she lifted herself up from the kneeler in front of her father's casket. I held out my hand and she latched onto it. I helped her to a chair in the first row next to her brothers and sister.

"Sorry about your dad."

I could tell she hadn't noticed who I was. Maybe my suit threw her off.

"Thanks," she said, dabbing her eyes with a tissue. "My dad and I were very close. I still can't believe..."

She rubbed her arms and rocked back and forth.

I waited until she was ready to talk.

"He was driving home from his job as an emergency medical technician. He saved a lot of people's lives, but nobody could save him."

"Can I get you anything like water or soda?"

"No, but maybe you can sit here for a while. This whole thing doesn't make sense. I don't know if it ever will."

Anna started crying, so I handed her the turquoise silk handkerchief Dad stuffed in my pocket.

"Pretty fancy snot rag," she said. All of a sudden, she started laughing hysterically. Her brothers and sister stared at her and frowned.

Dad once told me mourners sometimes experience extreme emotions and that laughing is good for them. He said a good funeral director accepts any feelings grieving people show and tries to be there for them.

She gave me the handkerchief back unused, rooted through her enormous handbag, and pulled out a wad of tissues.

"You look familiar. Do I know you from somewhere?"

I struck a pose like The Thinker. "Gym class? Cafeteria? The guy with the buzz cut and baggy pants outside the school?"

Anna studied my face. "You're the one I..."

"Make fun of? If that's what you were going to say, it's okay. I'm not scarred for life or anything."

She lowered her voice. "Sorry, I didn't mean to say those things."

Dad gave me the signal to circulate, so I got up. "If you need anything, just ask. I'll be here."

She started to fix the buttons on her jacket, which she'd buttoned wrong. "Will you be at the church tomorrow?"

"If you want me to."

She pointed out a woman in a purple dress who looked as old as Nonna. "Maybe you can look out for my mom. We can't talk to her. She's totally broken up."

"I'll definitely be there," I said.

I started moving among the people like Dad does and refilled the crystal candy dishes with mints and butterscotch.

A few minutes later, I was telling Dad about how I knew Anna from school, and his cell phone rang.

He made a face like he did when his migraines hit him. "Can you call back, Rayna? I'm working. No, Elliot can't talk now. He's helping me."

I could hear Mom making a complaining sound into the phone like the teacher in the Charlie Brown movie.

Dad fiddled with his tie. "Now's a bad time to come over. We're in the middle of a service."

Within fifteen minutes, Mom made her grand entrance in a black wool suit and the strand of genuine pearls Dad had given her on their tenth anniversary, just before they split up. Everyone stopped talking and turned to look at her.

She headed straight for Dad. "What's Elliot doing here? Does he know these people?"

Dad touched her shoulder. "I need to get back to the family. We'll talk later, Rayna."

"It's always later." She shooed him away like he was a pesky insect. "Anyway, I came to talk to Elliot, not you."

Dad wasn't about to argue. He could never win with Mom. "Okay, Rayna. I can spare him for a few minutes."

He walked over to Mrs. Santiago who was studying the framed pictures of her husband; one of their dream trip to the islands on a cruise ship; one of Anna her brothers and sister at an amusement park in Ocean City; and one of Mr. Santiago getting an award from the mayor for saving a firefighter's life.

I wondered how Dad dealt with people's sadness every day without becoming sad himself. Would I be able to do it?

Mom moved closer and put her arm around me. "Elliot, I've booked a suite at the Ritz so you could stay over. They have a fabulous café. Grab your overnight case."

"That won't work, Mom. I have to finish up here tonight, and I have to wake up early for the church service."

"You're working here tonight?" Mom asked like I was running a sting operation.

I tried to keep my voice down so people wouldn't hear. "Yes, and I'm going to do it whenever Dad needs help."

"You know how I feel about your being around this..."

"Business, Mom. It's a business like anything else. I enjoy helping people like Dad does. I think I may have a talent for it."

Mom's eyes filled with fire. "Would you like sticking a needle in a person, draining the blood and pumping embalming fluid through their veins? Is that how you want to spend your life?"

I loosened my tie. "I'm not sure yet. It's too early to tell. I know preparing bodies is a part of the job Dad's not crazy about. If I had to do it, I could. Science is my best subject. You have to learn about human anatomy in mortuary school."

"Then think about becoming a doctor like Grandpa Dan. You have the brains for it."

I looked over at the family and friends who were gathered near the casket for their final good-byes to Mr. Santiago. I had to get back to them soon.

"I have a long time to decide, Mom. For now, I hope you'll understand if I want to help Dad."

She looked like she did when her voiceover for Gas Away anti-flatulence tablets never made it to TV. "When can I see you again?"

"I'll call you tomorrow after the service. Maybe we can catch a movie."

She kissed me. The waxy imprint of her plum lipstick clung to my cheek. No matter how hard I tried, I couldn't rub it off.

Chapter Fourteen: Break a Leg

I was glad to get back to school on Monday. What a weekend. Nonna kept calling me a skeleton and tempting me to break my diet with her breaded pork chops, stuffed cheese potatoes, and triple-decker fudge brownies.

Mom said how it would break her heart if I became the fourth generation to operate The Carnucci Home for Funerals instead of being a cardiologist like her father, Grandpa Dan.

"I hope by the time I get back from LA again, you'll have given this more thought. By the way, that TV pilot didn't work out. They couldn't get enough sponsors. The good news is they're paying me a bundle to advertise drain cleaner."

Her voice rose to a high pitch like she wanted me to believe she was helping people by plugging the product. "This stuff works like magic with a plunger. You wouldn't have to pay a plumber a fortune to come out."

I couldn't resist the temptation. "Armand, the plumber, wouldn't like that."

Mom raised her eyebrow. "Don't worry, if he and your grandmother get serious, he'd never have to work again. Remember the killing she made in the stock market? Rigatoni and ravioli aren't the only things the old biddy excels at. Hopefully, that's not why Armand's chasing her."

I shuddered. "There's no way she'd marry him. Dad wouldn't let her."

"I don't think he'd have anything to say."

Without warning, tears formed in the corners of her eyes. "Do you think I've sold my soul?"

"You'd never do that," I said, but I secretly thought she might if the price was right.

~ * ~

The next day in homeroom, Ms. Begley passed around a sign-up sheet for school activities like newspaper, yearbook, and drama. I remembered that Rosalie had mentioned the school musical. Should I sign up, or was I wasting my time? I'd never been in a show before, but I could sing. When the paper reached my desk, I decided to sign my name.

A week later, Ms. Begley pulled a pile of letters from the office out of her homeroom book.

"I have call slips for those of you who signed up to join school activities. Elliot, we'll start with you." She handed me a sealed envelope with a happy and sad face logo, which meant only one thing, drama.

Canfield ripped the envelope from my hand. "What's this, 2K, an invitation to play Quasimodo, the ugliest guy on the planet?"

I grabbed Canfield's arm and struggled to get the letter back, but he buried it in his pocket and laughed. "You have to be quicker than that."

A crowd gathered around us.

I lunged toward Canfield. "Give it back now."

Two of Canfield's friends blocked my punch.

Canfield tossed the paper on the floor in front of me. "Go fetch, loser."

I grabbed the letter and stuffed it in my pocket.

Ms. Begley wrote up a pink slip, and gave Canfield five lunch detentions for disrupting homeroom. She also gave me detention for going after Kyle even though he'd started it. I didn't care. It was worth it.

I couldn't wait until the bell rang. I slipped into the library between classes to open my letter:

Dear Elliot,

You are invited to a drama club information session after school. You will learn about try-outs for "Man of La Mancha."
Break a leg.

Best regards,
Floyd Diggs, Drama Coach

I raced to the auditorium after my last class. Mr. Diggs paced in front of the stage as the kids worked on their one-act plays for assembly. He sprinted down the center aisle with his hand glued to his ear and looked up at the kids on stage.

"Can't hear you. If you don't want to bomb in front of the entire student body, you'll have to belt it out."

I almost plowed into Mr. Diggs on the way in, and the kids on stage screamed "Whoa," but not in a mean way. A few of them knew me from chorus. I guess they couldn't help but see how Kyle and his friends kept bugging me. A couple of them had even told Kyle to back off, but he warned them they'd be next if they didn't mind their business.

Mr. Diggs led me to a seat in the front row.

He clapped and everyone on stage quieted down. "Take a short break and be back here in ten minutes. When you get back, the key words are *loud* and *with feeling*. We want the audience to laugh and cry. We don't want them to doze off."

Everyone dashed out of the auditorium, and it was only Mr. Diggs and me.

He sat next to me on one of the auditorium chairs. He took up the whole seat and part of the one next to it. His coppery skin, wild Afro, and eyes the color of coal made him stand out in a crowd.

Mr. Diggs was one of those people you liked right away, before you even got to know them.

"The choir director told me you can belt out a song. We need good singers for the show. I'd like to see you try out."

"Maybe I will," I said in a laid back voice. I didn't want him to think I was too hungry for it.

He handed me a paper. "Here's an information sheet. Look it over and let me know if you can handle being in the show with all your other activities if you're picked. There's a lot of competition here. I hold practice five afternoons a week and all day Saturday."

Nobody at school knew, but I had CDs of all the Broadway shows. "Man of La Mancha" was one of my favorites. Every time I played the CDs, I sang along with them and knew all the words and music.

Rosalie told me the musical wasn't the actual "Man of La Mancha" they did on Broadway. The real show is about Aldonza, this sexy girl who goes out with a bunch of tough guys and gets a bad reputation.

She said Mr. Diggs had found a special version for younger kids, where Aldonza's a homeless person with family problems. That way, parents wouldn't complain about it being too wild for high school. They still kept all the songs from the original musical.

Did I have a chance to get one of the male parts? Most of the kids who got the leads had been in shows since they started middle school. I had the desire, which had to count for something.

Roy and I once watched this movie, "Stand and Deliver," about a teacher who turned kids who hated school on to learning. Everybody said those kids could never learn. The teacher in the movie said all you needed was *ganas,* desire, and you could get whatever you wanted in life.

All I wanted was to have Kyle stop bugging me. Getting a part in the musical would be a bonus. Would it happen if I wanted it enough and believed it would happen?

Chapter Fifteen: I Won't Tell

The day before spring break, I decided to stay in school late to do library research for science class. I had to write a paper identifying all the chemicals in my home and their possible side effects on humans.

My paper would probably be the longest in the class after I listed all the chemicals stocked in the funeral home. I'd read in the *Philadelphia Inquirer* about some middle school kids who were dumb enough to get high by soaking cigarettes in embalming fluid. One of them ended up dead. After that happened, Dad padlocked his chemicals.

The door near the gym was always open so kids who had after school activities could get out when they stayed late. Most of the other kids had left by now. I scooted down the hall, and I could hear some kids bouncing basketballs and shouting.

Suddenly, I found myself surrounded by Canfield and his friends: Bristow, Parker, Nevins, and Belser.

Canfield threw his ball to Bristow and moved in on me. "Stay after school to kiss up your teachers?"

Five against one. Did I have a chance? I held my hands out toward them, palms up. "Look, I don't want any trouble."

Canfield winked at the others and spun around to see if anyone was watching. Bristow threw the ball he was bouncing into one of the empty classrooms.

"Maybe we should get going, Kyle," Nevins said. He looked down the long hall toward Doc's office, but you'd need binoculars to see that far.

"Now might not be a good time."

Canfield grabbed him by the collar. "It's as good a time as any, Blake, unless you're going to wimp out on me."

The other guys looked like they'd been shot with a stun gun, paralyzed, unable to move. Finally, Belser bent down and tied his shoelace so I knew at least one of them hadn't been hypnotized.

Canfield pulled his grimy blue bandana with red stars off his head and tied it across my mouth. I tugged and pulled at it. Hard as I tried, I couldn't get it off. He must have won a medal in rope tying in Scouts, something I'd never been good at.

I threw fierce punches at Kyle, but he laughed and warded them off like I was an angry puppy trying to attack its powerful master.

"Lose a little of that blubber, 2K, and your fists might gain some power. You're not in shape like me, the invincible one," Kyle said.

I tried to scream "help" louder, but the bandana began to cut off my air supply, and I felt like I was suffocating.

Bristow came out of his trance. "We could get in big trouble for this, Kyle."

"You too?" Canfield roared. "Where's your loyalty, Jason? We're teammates and we're supposed to stick together."

"Yeah, but…"

"But nothing. One for all and all for one."

What were they planning to do to me? Had they all gone over the edge? I tried to scream, but all that came out from under the gag was *Mmmmmmmm.*

Most of the teachers and staff had already left to get an early start on spring break. Duke was probably somewhere in the building, though, giving the place a final once over before locking up. His doctor told him to slow down after the tests proved he had lung cancer, but it only made him work longer hours.

Kyle slammed me on the back. "Tell you what, promise not to open your mouth and I'll take the gag off."

I nodded *yes* like my head was going to roll off.

"Mmmmmmm..."

He untied the gag, and I heaved in a gulp of air.

"We don't want you to suffocate when your head hits the water."

Were they going to throw me in the river? Drown me? Could they be that crazy?

I tried to make a run for it, but Kyle caught me before I could make it to the door. His biceps bulged like baseballs from his lean arms. How I wished I'd added weight lifting to my fitness routine.

Canfield looked at his friends. "Part of the fun is the anticipation. Right, guys?"

Why couldn't they look at me?

I heard on the news that when you're threatened if you call a person by name, maybe he'll act more human and be less likely to hurt you. Was it worth a try?

"Kyle, you don't want to do this…"

I could tell he wasn't listening. His eyes were glazed over like he was a zombie.

"You can still stop this, Kyle. Let me go. I won't tell, I promise." I raised my hand like I was taking an oath.

"You're pathetic," he said. He tied the gag on me, tighter this time.

I started kicking and scratching like a wildcat. He gave his friends a signal.

They lifted me up and lugged me down the hall like I was a slab of beef.

Why were they stopping at the boys' room?

"Jason, you're the lookout. If you see or hear anybody, warn us."

"Okay," Jason said, but he started blinking like he had a tropical disease.

Canfield untied the gag and tossed it in the trash. They dragged me into the bathroom, banged open a stall, and pushed my head deep into the toilet. Canfield started flushing again and again until I thought I would drown.

At one point I heard Nevins say, "If he gets hurt, we're dead."

"If you can't take it, get out," Canfield said.

I started gagging from the pine smell of that blue stuff they put in the water. I remembered Nonna saying toilet bowl cleaners contained a lethal poison that could kill you.

Kyle yanked my head out of the bowl and dragged me to the full length mirror. The bowl cleaner had colored my head, face, and neck an eerie shade of blue.

Chunks of the taco salad I'd eaten at lunch spewed from my guts in spasms of throw up. I willed myself to stop, but the bitter smell of my own vomit made me puke more.

Kyle shook his head. "Look at yourself, loser. You're a total freak of nature."

Suddenly, my legs buckled and I dropped to the floor.

Canfield's friends stood there like they were in a coma, gaping at me. My eyes blurred from the blue stuff, but I could see enough to tell they didn't look like they enjoyed it.

Canfield pushed the door open. "We'd better split. Boardly, that custodian, is coming down the hall. He's worse than a cop."

"It wouldn't take much to beat up old Boardly," Bristow said.

Kyle gave him a slap on the shoulder. "Hey, I knew you'd come through."

"Don't hurt Duke…" I said, but my voice faded out.

They say the sense of hearing is the last thing to go. I wondered if I was dying. Somehow, I still managed to hear, but the voices sounded like they were talking underwater.

"Let's make a run for it," Canfield said. "Boardly moves like a snail with that mop and bucket. He'll never catch us."

"Stop," I screamed in my head, but the words stuck in my throat.

I could hear Duke yelling for them to stop. He shouted into his walkie. "Grady, they got Elliot. I dialed 911 for help. Those scoundrels are halfway down G-ramp."

"I've already caught them, Will. I'll hold them 'til Doc gets back. What'd they do this time?"

Through my hazy brain, I could make out Duke's face looking down at me. "Looks like they put him through some horrible water torture. Gotta go. Ambulance coming."

Duke's walkie blared static, then Grady came on. "Keep me posted, Will."

I tried to lift myself up, but my legs wouldn't cooperate, and I fell to the concrete floor, hitting my head. I lay there until my eyelids closed and I drifted into a deep sleep.

Chapter Sixteen: Something Happened

I felt someone touch my shoulder and smelled the same strong after-shave Dad wears. Only one other person I knew wore that scent.

"Wish you hadn't tried to stand up, and wish I could have caught you in time. Help will be here soon, son. Hang on." Duke paused after each word to take a breath.

He examined the lump on my head. "Those nasty, well, use your imagination to give those good-for-nothings' a name. Make it something you'd bleep out."

I tried to sit up, but Duke held up his hand, and I stayed on the hard, cold floor. "We have to make sure nothing's broken, so don't move 'til help gets here."

"How long have I been out?"

"Not long," Duke said. "I came as soon as I saw Kyle and his boys starting to take off down the hall. Doc had to leave early. He's testifying at a hearing to expel that kid that made a bomb threat last month. Grady called him, and he said to keep him informed."

I started shivering and Duke covered me with his old camouflage army jacket.

"I was supposed to pick up pizza. My grandmother and Dad must be wondering where I am."

Duke frowned. "I don't like that bump on your head, and I can see something made you sick."

He mopped up the pool of throw up surrounding me and wiped me off with his waxy cleaning rag.

What was that sound like a baby's cry coming from his chest? A wheeze–or something worse?

"You need to go to the hospital, but not to worry, son. I'll be with you."

I struggled to sit up. "No ambulance, I want to go home."

I was sure what happened would be all over school when we got back from spring break. If anybody in the area heard an ambulance siren, they'd think those guys had really gotten to me.

It was too late. I could hear the sharp screams of the ambulance. Before I could shout *stop*, a young male EMT and a woman about Mom's age shouted *one, two, three,* and hoisted me onto a stretcher. Then off we zoomed with Duke sitting next to me in the ambulance with its sirens wailing and lights blinking.

My head felt like a fizzy soda bottle about to pop, and everything spun around in front of me, including Duke, who looked like a midget one minute, and a colossal Frankenstein, the next. Was I having an anxiety attack, or did something happen to my brain when my head hit the ground?

Duke was on his phone again.

"Who are you calling?" I felt like somebody else was talking with my voice and I was outside my body watching some crazy movie.

"Lie back and rest," he said. "Try not to talk."

He turned away from me and lowered his voice. "This is Will Boardly from Bunche High School. Just to let you know, I've got Elliot here. Something happened at school, and we're on our way to the ER."

Duke put his hand over the phone. "Your grandmom is giving me an earful. She'll meet us at the hospital."

Duke took his hand away from the phone. "I don't think it's anything major, Mrs. Carnucci. Yes, he's conscious, but he needs to be checked out."

Duke brushed his head with the top of his hand. "Whew, she is one angry Granny. Don't want to be around when she butts heads with Doc.

Says she's going to sue the school."

"She always says that, but she never goes through with it. Did she say anything about my dad coming?"

Duke patted my arm. "Says he's in the middle of a memorial service for that young man on West Catholic's football team who passed suddenly."

When we arrived at St. Agnes Hospital, Nonna was pacing around the reception desk like a hyper cat.

They whisked me straight back to the ER, ahead of a wailing baby and a hunched over white-haired man clutching his stomach. The people in the waiting room stretched their necks to check me out. I must have looked like a Martian with my blue buzz cut. I was panting like I'd lifted one of Dad's caskets with a three-hundred-pound body in it.

As soon as they brought me into the ER cubicle, a technician jabbed me with a needle as long as a ruler and drew about twenty vials of blood.

The hospital assigned a resident, Dr. Ross Ginsberg, to my case. He said to call him Ross because he wasn't much older than me. I didn't feel comfortable doing that, so we settled on *Dr. Ross*.

Why was he writing so much on my chart? Was he going to make me stay here overnight? Finally, he looked up. "I'm going to order tests to see if you had a concussion from your fall."

By this time, Nonna had bulldozed her way into my cubicle. Duke said he'd wait right outside the room until the doctor gave him the word to come back in.

Dr. Ross talked to Nonna in a professional voice, like he'd been a doctor for forty years. "I'll let you know as soon as the test results come in. I'd appreciate it if you'd wait with Mr. Boardly until I finish examining Elliot."

Nonna looked at him like she did when she talked to Dad. "You'd better make it snappy, young man. I want to know what's wrong with my grandson."

He waited until Nonna went out into the hall. "Heard those boys gave you a swirly. When I was in school, all that meant was sticking a kid's head in the John and flushing a few times. Looks like they gave you the full treatment."

He put his stethoscope against my chest and wrote more on my chart, which was quickly becoming a thick book. "Bet that blue stuff tasted disgusting. Lucky you ingested a small amount or you'd need a stomach pump."

"You'd have to hold me down," I said.

He pinched the skin on my wrist. "You're dehydrated from throwing up. Even a little of that stuff can make you sick. I'm going to start an IV."

He stabbed the inside of my wrist with a needle to start the IV and told Nonna and Duke they could come back in.

"Be back to check on you, Elliot," Dr. Ross said as he flew out of the cubicle.

"I can't believe this happened," Nonna told Duke.

Duke patted her arm. "I'm concerned too, but I know he's going to come through this fine, Mrs. Carnucci."

"That's what you and that knucklehead vice principal said before. What does it take to get him to do something about those hooligans?"

Duke coughed into his handkerchief. "I'll call Doc tonight to give him the hospital report. He'll do something major this time, believe me."

A couple of hours later, Dr. Ross disconnected my IV. "Looks like all the tests came out normal. You'll have a little swelling from that lump, but it should go down in a few days, nothing to worry about."

I struggled to sit up. "When can I go home?"

Doctor Ross listened to my chest and ran his hand over the bump on my head. He scrawled something on my chart and looked up at me. "How does tonight sound?"

I felt like leaping out of that lumpy hospital bed. "You mean it?"

He nodded. "I'd like you to rest up, take a short vacation from school, maybe a few days more after spring break."

I didn't mean to sound whiny, but I couldn't help it. "I want to go back when everyone else goes back. It will be worse if I don't."

Dr. Ross smiled. I could tell he cared about me. "I can understand why you feel that way, but I think it's best to let your body and mind heal a little before you go back. You've been through quite an ordeal."

No way was I going to stay home with Nonna bugging me to *mangia, mangia, eat, eat* every minute and giving me the third degree like a police interrogator. I didn't feel like arguing, so I said, "I'll think about it."

Doctor Ross glanced at my chart and back at me. "I'll call you at home in a few days to see how you're doing. Meanwhile, take care."

"Thanks," I said.

We shook hands, and he sped around the corner to see his next patient.

From outside in the hall, I could smell Mom's musky perfume. How did she get here so fast, and how would I deal with Nonna and her in the same room?

Nonna stuck her nose in the air, and looked her up and down. "Rayna, I thought you were in California."

Mom shimmied out of her black wool poncho and dropped her red beaded purse on my bed. "That's a fine welcome, Angela."

"We meet again," Mom said holding out her hand to Duke. "In case you forgot, I'm Rayna."

"No, no. I definitely remember. I may be old but I'm not addled. Wish we could have gotten reacquainted under better circumstances."

Mom propped herself on the stool next to my bed.

Was it possible to be happy to see someone and annoyed at her at the same time? Mom popped in and out of my life whenever it was convenient for her, and yet I hated when she wasn't around. Did she know how she made me feel?

"Who told you? How did you get here so fast?" I said.

"My plane got in this afternoon. I went to the house hoping to surprise you. Nobody even thought to call me. I found your father in the middle of a service. I thought he'd never escape that long-winded preacher. Andrew told me what happened and said he'd get here as soon as he could."

Nonna shook her finger at Mom. "You should talk, Rayna. You come and go as you please and leave your son to fend for himself."

"Don't judge me, Angela. You're the reason I left in the first place."

Nonna narrowed her eyes at her, and Mom backed off.

Duke clapped his hands like he was a teacher calming a rowdy class. "Maybe it would be best for us to wait in the lobby."

"Who are you to tell us what to do?" Mom asked, studying Duke's holey jeans and faded Phillies cap.

Duke answered like the president at a press conference. "I am the head custodian, and I'm in charge here."

Mom flashed her blinding dental implants at him. "O–*kay*, since you put it that way."

Nonna said Armand, the plumber, was bringing her a Poo Poo Platter all the way from the Hong Kong Pearl in Bucks County and that she'd be honored if Duke would join them at the Carnucci Funeral Home for a late dinner. After all, he'd rescued her grandson.

"I'd love to. Haven't eaten all day."

He got this sly look in his eye. "Don't want to cause trouble, but can we invite Rayna? I think she'd enjoy the Poo Poo Platter too."

What was he thinking?

Mom buttoned her poncho and grabbed her purse. "I've had enough poo poo for one day. I don't think it's a good idea."

"Oh, why not?" Nonna said. "We all want the same thing, to see Elliot happy."

"You do?" I asked.

Nonna got a fishy look in her eye like she did when she cheated at poker. "Before we leave, I have some good news."

Was she thinking of moving into a life care community with Mrs. O'Reilly?

"You're going to stop snooping on me?"

Nonna gave me a slight frown. I guess she was too worried about me to give me her look that could shrivel you into a Lilliputian. "I've already told Andrew my news, but he didn't take it very well."

"What?" Mom, Duke and I shouted in a chorus.

The ninety-five-year-old man in the next cubicle, who'd been asleep the whole time I was there, pulled back the curtain surrounding his bed with his shaky hand and turned up his hearing aid.

Nonna shouted as if she'd just won the lottery. "Armand and I are getting engaged in a couple of months."

"Whoopi-do," the man next to us shouted. "You go, Grandma."

She gave him an icy stare. "Go back to sleep, Grandpa," she said.

"Not on your life. This is better than a TV sitcom."

The thought of gorilla face being my grandfather gave me chills. "I thought you and Armand were friends. You just met him."

"True, but when you're my age, you don't know how many more years you have. Living among the dead has taught me that."

Nonna was getting older, but I thought she had good sense until now.

"Marrying Armand might be worse than living with dead people," I said.

Nonna opened her mouth to throw a zinger back at me, but Mom interrupted her. "I'm not trying to top you, Angela, but I have an announcement too."

"This has been some night," Duke said, tapping his chest. "Too much excitement for this old ticker." He looked at the elderly man in the next bed, who was still straining to hear us. "I might have to steal your bed, sir."

The man grinned. "You can take the top bunk."

"I've decided to move back to Philly," Mom said.

I didn't know if her news made me happy or sad. "You moved to LA only four months ago. Your career is taking off."

"Yes, but being out there by myself I realized I'm missing out on seeing you grow up, especially now that this happened. I can always find work here, something more meaningful like teaching. That's what I studied in college. When you're caught up in all that glitz and glitter, you miss out on the important things in life."

"This *is* a surprise," Nonna said.

Was this Mom talking? I'd never known her to want to change the way she lived. I thought her career meant everything to her. Somehow, I couldn't see her wrestling with a class full of rowdy kids.

"Have you told Dad?"

"He thinks it's a great idea. You and I can spend more time together."

Was it really going to happen or if it was another of Mom's fantasies? I'd learned to be a little skeptical of what the adults in my family told me. That way I wouldn't be too disappointed if they didn't follow through.

Nobody said anything for a long time, but Mom broke the silence.

"I want you to know I'm happy for you, Angela," Mom said to Nonna and gave her a small hug. To my surprise, Nonna didn't tell her to back off.

I was beginning to think Nonna was right when she said everything happened for a reason. Would Mom and Nonna have gotten along, even for a minute, if I hadn't ended up in the hospital?

Mom put her hand on mine. "I'm going to go back to my hotel, but your dad will be here soon. If you'd like, Duke, I'll drop you off at your house. Maybe your daughter can give you a ride to the Carnucci's later for dinner."

"Sounds good. It's been a long night for everyone."

He patted my back. "Good night, son. Take care."

~ * ~

A few minutes later, Dad showed up to take me and Nonna home.

Dad wore jeans and a blue and white striped shirt rather than his usual three-piece suit and tie, which made him look like Lurch from the old Adams Family TV show.

"Sorry I'm late," he said, and hugged me. I thought he'd never let go.

He sat down next to me. "You know, son, I want to say I'm sorry for not spending much time with you lately. I get so caught up in work..."

I waved him away. "It's okay, Dad. Besides, having Nonna hovering over me every minute is about all I can take."

It was a good thing Nonna couldn't hear me. She was sleeping with her mouth open and totally out of it.

Dad looked at me. "No, son, it's not okay. I want to spend more time doing things together, for me as much as for you. Everything that's happened has made me do a lot of thinking. I want you to know I'm hiring a new assistant and a couple of recent mortuary school grads to take up the slack, so I can find more balance in my life. Aida has decided to retire and start a catering business, which is more her thing than looking after the dead."

"I'm glad, Dad. Maybe we can take in some Phillies games."

He brushed away a couple of stray tears. "Sounds good. I can't wait."

I was starting to feel weird hearing Dad tear up and talk like that, so I asked him if he'd talked to anyone at school about what happened.

"As a matter of fact, I have some news. Doctor Greely called to give me an update. He and the school board are pushing for Canfield to be expelled. This will make Canfield and his family madder than pit bulls, but they have that friend on the school board who might try to help them. Doctor Greely is also giving the other kids a two-week suspension from school, plus they were all thrown off the team."

I should have been happy, but I felt numb, like I couldn't bear to think about what happened and what was going to happen. I wanted it all to be over.

Dad inspected the bump on my head and rested his hand on my shoulder. "Doctor Greely thinks it's best if you stay home for a few days after the break until things blow over. LeBron and Roy offered to pick up your assignments."

"I'm going back to school as soon as I can."

Nonna bolted awake, and Dad and Nonna locked eyes. "We'll talk about it, but Nonna might have other ideas."

Nonna's lips tightened into a straight line. "You're darned right I do."

A wave of anger washed over me. "I don't care what anybody thinks. I have to start making my own decisions."

I could see a tear forming in Nonna's eye, but then her jaw hardened and she morphed into her tough old self again.

Dad handed me a fresh change of clothes. "We'll talk to Dr. Ross again in a few days and see if he's changed his mind."

I wished they'd stop trying to run my life.

I pulled on my jeans and sweatshirt. I hoped nobody had seen my bare butt hanging out in that goofy gown. It was the one part of my body I still couldn't reduce.

"Can we go home now?"

"Good idea. Stick around a hospital long enough and you'll really get sick." Nonna pumped a squirt of antibacterial soap from the wall dispenser and rubbed her hands like Lady Macbeth.

She grabbed her oversized tote bag that held everything from casino chips to laxative powder.

"I'll bring the car around," Dad said.

A volunteer helped me into a wheelchair, and we got onto the elevator with Nonna.

"I have some leftover turkey noodle soup for you at home," Nonna said.

"I want the Poo Poo Platter."

"Maybe just a little," she said.

I was too weak to argue, so I eased into the front seat of the dead wagon, and Dad pulled out of the hospital lot.

Chapter Seventeen: My Destiny Calls

It turns out I couldn't eat much of my Poo Poo platter, or even cashew chicken, my favorite. That blue toilet bowl stuff definitely dampened my appetite. Maybe that was a good thing.

I was amazed at how great Mom and Nonna got along, or pretended to, probably because Duke was there and they didn't want to look dumb in front of him.

After we ate, I couldn't keep my eyes open, so I plodded up the stairs and went right to sleep. Nightmares of Canfield dunking my head in the toilet haunted me all night.

A few days later, after spring break had ended, Nonna rapped on my door. We'd talked to Dr. Ross who said he didn't see any harm in my going back to school after I'd rested up a couple more days. It's a good thing because with Dad, Nonna, and Mom hovering over me, I couldn't wait to get out of the house.

"You've got visitors," Nonna said.

"I don't want to see anyone," I shouted in my rudest voice.

She banged on my door so hard I thought it would cave in. "Your friends aren't leaving. If you're thinking you look a mess, you're right. But friends don't care about that stuff."

It didn't matter what I wanted because Nonna threw open my door. If it had been locked, she would have probably broken it down.

Before I could get up, Roy and LeBron burst into my room, dropped a bucket of fried chicken and a bag of biscuits on my night table, and dumped my school books and the assignments I'd missed on the floor.

My hair was shaggy and I had on a torn up pair of pajamas, but they didn't seem to notice. I guess Nonna was right about that one thing.

There was no stopping them, so I grabbed a chicken leg, dipped it in honey mustard, and gnawed on it like a starving lion. My diet was the last thing on my mind. After all, I'd puked my guts out and must have lost a few pounds not eating anything but toast and ginger ale for a few days afterwards.

LeBron sat on the side of my bed. "Thought you'd want to know they're working on expelling Canfield."

"Canfield's dad's buddy on the school board won't be able to save him this time," Roy said.

LeBron laughed. "They'll kick his butt good."

Roy snatched a small cherry pie out of the bag. "Doc says he's going to push for an anti-bully program in all the schools in our district."

"You might have to testify," LeBron said. "If you told first-hand what happened, they'd probably go for the plan."

I wiped my greasy chicken hands on my pajama bottoms. "Dad said Kyle's lawyer wants me to go to his expulsion hearing to talk about what happened. He says the people in charge might let him back in school if he apologizes. It kind of gives me a creepy feeling seeing him after what happened."

"Why?" LeBron asked. "You're the man at school now."

"What do you mean?" I asked, pushing away the pie Roy waved in my face.

"You're the guy who might get Canfield expelled. Then he won't be able to bother anybody else."

Roy broke off a chunk of his pie and gave the other half to LeBron. "I hear his dad wants him to go to military school if they kick him out."

LeBron saluted us. "He won't be able to mess with anybody there."

Ray jammed the pie in his mouth and gulped it down. His gigantic Adam's apple swelled and then relaxed like a camel's.

"Is your Dad going to press charges?"

"He's going to see what happens at the hearing. We figure if Canfield gets expelled, that's a good enough punishment."

LeBron let out a big sigh. Could he actually be full?

"The best punishment he could get, man. The most important thing to him is that everybody sees him as the most popular guy in school and the best athlete. He'll be a nobody if he gets kicked out for good."

I gathered up my clothes so I could get out of my pajamas. "I want to stop thinking about Kyle."

LeBron smiled. "You've got try-outs to look forward to, and things are looking up."

I went into the bathroom and threw on ragged jeans and a band t-shirt.

After I got dressed, I sat on the floor next to Roy and LeBron. "I've been thinking about something Duke said."

Roy handed me his dirty comb, and I tossed it back to him like it was a scorpion.

"Something he said in that letter he sent you?" LeBron asked.

I looked in the mirror and tried to make myself presentable. "He mentioned helping other kids who were going through the same thing I have. I've been thinking maybe I can start a club to help kids at school deal with the kind of stuff I've had to live with these past few months."

Roy started cleaning up our mess. "Hey, I've been there too. Count me in."

LeBron looked like a light bulb went off in his head. "We could have the first meeting at your house. A lot of kids would show up. They're all curious about what it's like to live in a funeral home."

Roy smiled "Yeah, maybe offer tours, and charge for them."

"We'd have to draw a big crowd if we wanted to split it three ways," LeBron said.

I flopped into my desk chair. I was up only a short time, and my eyes were starting to droop. "Seriously, guys, maybe we can get other kids involved, kids from different crowds, who want to help."

"Good idea," Roy said. "My mom's a teacher, and she told me

about research they're doing on bullying and how powerful the kids witnessing bullying are. They call them bystanders."

"We'll talk about it soon," I said.

LeBron tapped my back. "We're with you, buddy."

Chapter Eighteen: Whatever is, *is*.

By the time drama try-outs came up, the kids at school had pretty much stopped talking about "the episode."

But word was getting around I was going to face Canfield and his father at the hearing where they were going to decide whether to kick Kyle out of our school permanently.

I was glad the play try-outs were coming up. They gave me something other than the hearing to think about. Five guys, including me, were auditioning for Don Quixote, and most of them had experience in the drama club. Mr. Diggs said everyone had an equal chance whether they were long time performers or new ones. He didn't guarantee anyone a part because they'd had one before.

I'd made my goal of losing forty pounds, but I still didn't look as scrawny as Don Quixote on try-out day. When Mr. Diggs sat down at the piano and played, I closed my eyes and psyched myself up to get into the part. That's what Mom does when she auditions for commercials.

I looked past Mr. Diggs, past the other kids trying out, and belted out Don Quixote's part from "Man of La Mancha" about how his destiny calls and how he's ready to go wherever it takes him.

Man, was I sweating. Did I bomb or did they like me? I had no way of knowing.

Mr. Diggs said he'd be in touch and started packing up his music. I wish I could have read his mind, but his face gave me no clue what he was thinking.

The next day Ms. Begley gave me a note in homeroom. I crossed my fingers and ripped it open.

Dear Elliot,

You are invited to a call back tomorrow on stage after school for the role of Don Quixote. Bring your script and music.

Best regards,

Floyd Diggs

I wondered who else he'd called back. Could I beat out someone who had more experience, or would I have to wait until next year to try out again?

When I got to the auditorium, Carlos Watson was already on stage rehearsing the part of Don Quixote with one of the prompters. He saw me and stopped in the middle of his song. "Looks like it's between you and me."

"I saw you in 'South Pacific' last year. You did an amazing job."

Carlos smiled. "Thanks, but this role's a little harder. You've got to hit those high notes, and I see myself as more of an actor than a singer."

Mr. Diggs hustled up the stage steps, and everyone got quiet.

The call back took a few minutes, shorter than I'd expected, but I felt more exhausted than when I worked a three-hour visitation for Dad. Carlos had done a great job of hitting the high notes, but so had I.

"This is going to be a tough decision," Mr. Diggs said after we both sang our guts out. "I'll post who got the parts outside the English office tomorrow at eight AM sharp."

I didn't want to waste any time thinking about how Carlos knew what he was doing and how I didn't have a chance against him. Instead, I concentrated on what Duke told me the last time we talked: "Act as if you've made it, and you will." If things didn't work out, I knew I'd done my best. That counted for something.

~ * ~

The next day I got to school early and rushed to the English office to check out the bulletin board. I looked at the three lead parts for Cast A, the one that gave the most performances:

Dulcinea: Rosalie Giordano; Sancho Panza: Tomás Blanco; and Don Quixote: Elliot K. Carnucci

DON QUIXOTE: ELLIOT K. CARNUCCI!

I ran out into the hall, gave a wild yelp, and leaped in the air like a pole-vaulter. Ms. Williams ran out of her room.

"Elliot, there are classes in session. What's all this noise?" I guess she hadn't seen the posting.

I was breathing hard and had a hard time getting the words out. "I made it. I got the lead."

She took my hand between both of hers and squeezed it. "I always thought you were star material. I'll make an announcement in class today."

"Okay, if you want to," I said.

I'd never liked to call attention to anything I did before, but today I felt different. Getting the part made me happy and proud, but not in a conceited way. *Grateful* was more the word.

Later that afternoon I showed up at Kyle's expulsion hearing with Dad, dressed in the suit I wore to the Santiago service. We had it dry-cleaned because it reeked of carnations and gardenias from the reposing room. Nonna wanted to go too, but I didn't think we could take a chance with her and Kyle's family in the same room.

The fact that I'd gotten the part sort of took the edge off having to face Kyle and tell my side of the story. I didn't know what to expect, but I was prepared for anything. Duke always said, "Whatever is *is*. There's nothing you can do about it, so make the best of it."

We took the speed elevator to the school superintendent's office. Ms. Klein, Kyle's lawyer, shook my hand, thanked me for coming, and told us it wouldn't take long. Ms. Browne, a representative from the school board, explained she and the superintendent would preside over the hearing and would decide whether Kyle would be expelled from Bunche High School or would be allowed back in school. His attorney was here at his parents' request and would help Kyle if he needed it.

The superintendent of schools was a tall, slim woman with short, flaming red hair. She told me to relax and to do my best to remember what happened. "I want you to explain all the events that resulted in your injury. We've read reports from your teachers, Doctor Greely, Mr. Boardly, and the doctor at the hospital. Now we want to hear from you, Elliot."

She and the school board president asked me a ton of questions about when the bullying started and how it got worse. I answered the best I could. When I was finished, I felt drained but not beaten down.

Kyle looked over at me a couple of times while I was telling what happened. Was he wondering how he could weasel out of the charges, or was he silently plotting his next move against me? You could never tell with him.

I nodded at Canfield's parents. I don't think they recognized me from when they were in Doc's office, but I avoided Kyle's eyes. He had on new khakis, and his muscles bulged like oranges underneath his Bunche basketball shirt. His hair looked as shaggy as a sheep dog's.

Dad looked him over. "So this is the kid who's made your life hell," he whispered. "Good thing Nonna isn't here."

"Yeah, she'd probably curse him out in Italian."

Dad winked at me. "Maybe smack him around."

Ms. Klein turned to Kyle. "We've invited Elliot here because you have something to say to him."

He stood there like an automaton, and Mrs. Canfield said, "*Kyle*?"

Kyle looked away. "Yeah, well I…"

His dad squeezed his arm. "You agreed to apologize, I expect you to keep your word."

I saw Dad chewing on his lip the way he did when he wanted to tell somebody off.

No matter how hard Kyle tried, he couldn't meet my eyes. "Sorry," he finally said. "I never wanted it to go this far, but once I started, I couldn't stop. I don't know why I did it..."

Ms. Klein put her hand on Kyle's shoulder and turned to me. "Do you have anything to say to Kyle now that he's apologized?"

I let out a breath and looked in his empty eyes. "I hope you never do this to anyone again, and I hope you learned something from it. I know I did."

Kyle looked at me for few seconds, but he didn't say anything. Had he grinned at me, or was it my imagination? I wondered if he'd apologized so the superintendent and the school board would go easy on him and forget about expelling him. Or could he have meant what he'd said?

~ * ~

The next day a few kids gathered around me in homeroom. "We heard what happened at the hearing," one of the kids said. "My dad said he read in the paper that Kyle's parents are definitely sending him to Brighten Military Academy if he gets expelled."

Later, I met up with Roy and LeBron in the hallway. They wanted to talk about celebrating my getting a part in the show. I told them I'd catch them later because Doc wanted to see me right away.

I hustled to Doc's office. He motioned for me to sit down until he finished his phone call. I squirmed in my seat. "What's going on? Am I in trouble?" I asked when he finally put down the phone.

He stared at a spot on the wall. "I'm sorry to tell you Duke is in the hospital. His heart problem, the atrial fibrillation, is very serious."

"That can't be. I just talked to him yesterday."

Doc studied the papers on his desk. "His daughter called. He's asking for you."

"Do you have his number?"

"You might want to see him in person. His daughter says he's taken a downward turn with the cancer, and his heart problem is compounding it." He looked down at the floor. "That can happen in cases like his."

I put my head in my hands, rocked back and forth and started to cry, not caring that Doc saw. Then I jumped up and bolted out of the office.

"Elliot..." he called after me. I turned around, and he looked like he was crying too, but I couldn't go back. I felt like screaming the worst words in the world. As Duke always says, "Like something you'd bleep out."

Chapter Nineteen: A Good Life

After I left Doc's office, I took the Broad Street subway to Temple Hospital. I didn't have an umbrella, and I got soaked from the sudden storm.

The receptionist wore a bright pink jumper over a white blouse and a big button that read *Alice Herron, 15 years of service*. She had her eyes glued to one of those tabloids with a picture of Jesus appearing in the sky with a mushroom cloud in the background. The headlines read *The World is Coming to an End: How to Prepare for the Last Days.*

I was panting hard from running. "I'm here to see Mr. William Boardly."

She flipped the page of her magazine. "Sorry, I can only admit immediate family members to the intensive care unit."

"He's my friend, and I'm not leaving until I talk to him."

Ms. Heron stuffed her magazine in her handbag and finally looked up. "Let me see what I can do."

I guess she felt sorry for me with water dripping from every crevice of my body because she didn't waste any time calling upstairs.

"The ICU nurse says you can go on up."

Up in the ICU, nurses and doctors sat on swivel chairs behind a long table, their eyes glued to screens. Monitors registered patients' vital signs. The smell of disinfectant mingled with body fluids made me woozy.

A short man with a wide smile put his hand out, and I shook it. "I'm Calvin Epps, Mr. Boardly's nurse. He's expecting you. I'm sorry to say he's not doing well. His daughters are taking it hard, probably feeling guilty because they haven't spent time with him over the years."

He walked me down the hall. "All we can do at this point is keep him comfortable. He wants to go home, and that's what we're aiming for."

Calvin stopped outside a room with a sign that read *ICU, William Walker Boardly*. Seeing his full name like that hit me hard, and a chill ran through me. It looked cold and formal, like when Dad posts the dead persons' names outside the reposing rooms. Nobody is ever known by nicknames there. But come to think of it, putting *Duke* on the sign would have looked pretty dumb.

"How long does he have?" I asked.

"Nobody knows for sure, but Mr. Boardly's a fighter, so you never know. His A-fib's been acting up, which, at this point, is our major concern."

I could feel my heart racing. I hated not knowing what to expect.

Duke lay in his bed, hooked up to a maze of hoses, bottles and tubes. I looked up at the monitor and could see that his blood pressure and heart rate had soared.

Two women dressed in business suits, one navy and one grey, stood on either side of him. I figured they were twins because they looked exactly alike, with their heart-shaped faces and highly arched eyebrows.

The one in the navy spoke first. "I'm Tara Stiles, and this is my sister, Tanya Biggins."

Duke's face had a pasty caste to it, almost like the corpses I saw before Aida restored them with her magic fluids and Mazie transformed them with her make-up kit. I'd seen a lot of dead bodies, but I couldn't stand the thought of someone I cared about dying.

Duke nodded at me and smiled faintly, but he was sweating and breathing heavily so I guess it was hard for him to talk.

Tanya motioned for her sister and me to come out to the hallway. Duke followed me with his eyes.

"Dad speaks very highly of you. He told me about your part in the show. Do you want to be a professional actor?"

"Actually I'm thinking of becoming a funeral director."

After I said it, I could have kicked my own butt for saying something so dumb. I'm sure that was the last thing they wanted to hear with their father lying in a hospital bed in critical condition.

Tanya smiled at me and then looked at her sister. "Tara considered going to mortuary school until we went on a field trip to a funeral home."

"The visit to the embalming room was the main thing that made me change my mind," Tara said. "The needles, blood and chemical smells almost bowled me over. The teacher had to rush me out of there before I passed out."

I didn't know what to say, their talking about death and all when Duke was in the next room, so I started telling them how their father had helped me deal with some major bullying problems at school.

"That's how he was when we were growing up," Tanya said. "If he'd had the chance to go to college, he might have become a teacher or a psychologist."

Tanya looked toward Duke's room. "I think I hear Dad. Tara and I will wait in the lounge down the hall. Why don't you go in?"

I felt like bolting. I didn't want to see him this way, but I crept into the room.

They had shaved off Duke's beard, and I could see deep creases around his lips, pulling his mouth downward, making him look like he'd aged ten years. He was wearing a flimsy hospital gown with yellow daisies that tied in the back.

"Come here, son," he said, reaching for my hand. "Do an old man a favor, will you? Don't let that Pablo chop off your hair anymore."

I took off my baseball hat so he could see my hair was starting to look like the short crew cuts the football players wear.

"It's starting to grow in nicely now," he said. "I went to Pablo once, and he made me look like a bald eagle."

I poured him a cup of ice water, and he sipped it slowly from a straw.

"I'm going to take your suggestion about helping other kids."

He nodded. "You're turning something bad into something good."

"It was your idea."

"You're going to make it happen, and that's what counts."

A smile played around his lips. "Tanya told me about the article in the paper, how you spoke up for yourself at the hearing."

"I'm glad it's over. I still don't believe it happened."

I could barely hear him. "Things are getting better..."

"I hope so." I moved closer to him. "The nurse said they want to send you home soon."

He chuckled. "I guess they think the end is near."

"Don't talk that way. Nobody knows how much time they have."

His arm was blue from the IV, and he was fidgeting around in his bed, trying to get comfortable. "I've lived a good life, son. I may not be the richest man in town, but people like you, friends I've met, have brought me happiness. My wife and I had many good years, and we had two daughters who have careers they love. What more could I want?"

"I guess when you put it that way..."

He looked at me for a long minute, like he was taking a picture of my face. I felt like I was going to crack, but I thought of something goofy, like Nonna kissing Armand with that bushy mustache, and I snapped back.

"I want to talk about the kind of service I want," he said suddenly. "I don't want a viewing, only a memorial service. Knowing how adventurous your dad is, he'd want to lay me out looking like Little Richard, that wild oldies singer, and play 'Good Golly, Miss Molly' on that famous sound system of his."

"I wouldn't let that happen. I'll write down your instructions and be sure everything's done the way you want it."

"I'd appreciate that," he said.

He breathed in and took forever to exhale. "Could you do it now?" he asked.

I swallowed hard. "If that's what you want, sure."

I grabbed a pen from the clipboard that held Duke's chart and wrote on the back of an old menu.

I headed the page "Duke's Last Wishes" like I was one of Dad's official funeral pre-planners.

I guess Duke didn't want his daughters to deal with the zillion and one details people have to after somebody dies, like open or closed casket, cremation, in the ground or mausoleum, or mainly, what to spend for the final send-off.

It was hard for Duke to talk and it took forever, but it was worth it because it was something he really wanted to do.

Here's exactly how Duke's list looked when we finished:

The Last Wishes of William Walker Boardly, AKA Duke

1. No gaping at me after I'm gone, just me with the lid closed and a picture on top, the one with me and my wife, Theresa, and the girls jumping the waves on the beach.

2. I want music. As you know, I love music, especially doo wop music. Lighten things up by playing "School Days" by Chuck Berry. After all, Bunche High School's where I spent my best years.

3. I want you to sing "How Great Thou Art," Elliot. Don't overdo the Holy Roller stuff 'cause I'm just an ordinary guy trying to do the best he can with what he's got. Whatever you do, for the very last number, play "Duke of Earl." That's how I want everyone to remember me, as my Lady's Duke 'cause those were the best years of my life.

4. Bury me next to Miss Theresa, and skip the flowers. I'm allergic.

5. I'm leaving a little money to throw a small bash at Aldo's Bar and Grill by invitation only as I don't have a lot of cash to spare. You can choose five students. Definitely include Roy and LeBron. My daughters can pick the forty people they think I'd most want to be there. Be sure they invite Doc, Grady, the cop, and, of course, your entire family. Don't forget about Nonna and her beau.

Signed, sealed, and delivered,
William Walker Boardly, AKA, Duke

He insisted on signing it even though his hand shook so much he could barely hold the pen.

I turned to look out the window. I could see the people racing to take the subway home from work. The sun had disappeared behind charcoal clouds, and hailstones, the size of baseballs thumped against Duke's window, rattling the panes. Duke didn't seem to notice.

"I wish I could do something to help make you better," I said.

He reached for my hand. "You have. You've been my friend. That's the best thing you can do. By the way, I heard you got the lead in the school show. Break a leg for me."

The room smelled moldy and musty like our basement. Outside, in the distance, a police siren wailed.

"The school show's coming up soon. You'll be home way before then. I'll bring you a video."

"I'm looking forward to seeing it," he said. "I'm not going anywhere for a while, at least, not if I have anything to say about it."

"Better not," I said.

I raced out the door. I didn't want him to see me bawl.

Chapter Twenty: What We Do For Each Other

That night Duke came to me in a dream. He was dressed in a white sport coat and khakis, and his Sixers hat had the visor turned around like a kid would wear it. I couldn't see his face, but I knew it was Duke.

He and his wife, who'd died about twenty years ago, were walking the boardwalk in Atlantic City. They were holding hands, and Duke was saying how it reminded him of when the kids were little and they took a trip to the beach every Sunday.

"Takes me back to the good times we had, Duke," his wife said. "Only thing missing is our girls."

He put his arm around her. "They have their own lives now, Theresa. We have to let them go." He smiled at her like she was the only person on earth. "Besides, we're together again now."

They headed toward an arcade where you could win stuffed alligators and elephants if you got all the balls in a basket. Duke threw one of the balls, and it made the basket.

"Not to worry, Theresa. We'll see the girls again," he said, and his wife smiled.

Suddenly, Duke turned around, and I could see his face. What the heck. He didn't have a wrinkle, and he breathed like a normal person. He started singing "The Duke of Earl" but this time he wasn't humming. He was singing the words to his wife like one of those a cappella crooners from back in the day.

At six AM, my cell blasted me out of my coma-like sleep.

"'Lo," I said in my grumpiest voice.

"Elliot, this is Tara Stiles, Duke's daughter."

Why was she calling me now? Was Duke okay?

"I hesitated calling this early, but I thought you'd want to know. In the middle of the night, Daddy suffered a serious bout of rapid heartbeat. The doctors worked on him for a long time…"

"He's okay, isn't he? I was just talking to him."

Ms. Stiles began to sob, and I could barely understand her.

"Daddy passed at five thirty this morning of a stroke. His heart gave out, and, of course, the cancer had weakened him."

"No," I said, starting to cry myself. "Tell me it's not true. I knew he was sick, but I didn't think it would happen yet. He said he wasn't going anywhere for a while."

"I think he may have had a premonition. A couple of hours after you left, he said he heard our mother calling him, and he said, 'Theresa, don't be calling me yet. I'm not ready to leave.'"

More than a few of Dad's families had told him the same thing, that before their loved ones died, they mentioned a relative who had gone before calling them.

"He was like a grandfather to me," I said.

Ms. Stiles stopped crying, but her voice sounded low and flat, almost like a robot. "He loved you like a grandson. I was glad he had you because my sister and I weren't about to have babies any day soon."

I didn't know how to say it, so I just came out with it. "He gave me a list of what he wanted done."

"Yes," she said. "Daddy told me about it after you left. Please e-mail it to me, so I can start planning the arrangements. I've already called your father, and he has everything under control. That means a lot to us."

"I'll do whatever I can to help. I'll see you at the service."

After I hung up, I felt like my body was stuck to the bed and that I'd been hit with a paralyzing laser ray that froze my body.

I was struck back into reality by the sounds of Nonna outside my door, coughing and sneezing, like she always does on her way to the bathroom in the morning.

"Heard you talking on the phone. You sounded stressed."

She plopped herself on my bed. My head fell into my hands, and I couldn't look at her. Couldn't she see I needed to be alone?

Nonna put her face up in mine so I was forced to look at her. She didn't have her false teeth in yet, so she talked with a lisp, but I could still understand her. There's no stopping Nonna when she wants to say something.

I looked past her to avoid her eyes, so I wouldn't cry. "Duke died."

Nonna ran her hand over her forehead. "What a bummer, but I can't say I'm surprised with his lungs and that heart problem."

"I didn't want it to happen so soon."

"Me neither, but you, better than anyone, know that death takes people when it wants to. That's why we've got to make every day count for something and tell people how we feel about them while they're still around. You can feel good knowing you did that with Duke."

I knew what she said was true, but it all sounded like one big, bad cliché, and I didn't want to think about it now. All I wanted was to see Duke walking down the hall in his faded jeans and baseball cap.

When I clammed up, Nonna finally got the hint and left.

~ * ~

At breakfast that morning, Dad hugged me hard before he sat down to Nonna's sausage and pancakes. "I'm so sorry to hear about Mr. Boardly. I know how hard this must be for you."

When he let go, I could see traces of tears in his eyes. Even though he has to deal with death every day, it still gets to him, especially when it's someone he's met and cared about.

Dad said he thought it would help me deal with Duke's death better if I had a part in his service. He wanted me to greet the guests like I did at the Santiago funeral and to pay particular attention to Duke's daughters by doing whatever I could to make them comfortable.

Dad said Mom would fly in for the funeral. I remembered how the day we ate the Poo Poo Platters, Duke had made her laugh. Usually, Mom wasn't one to lighten up, especially with someone she barely knew, but she giggled when Duke told her how he was probably the only guy in history who'd picked "Duke of Earl" as a wedding song.

The morning of the memorial, Mario, the singing barber, plunked himself down at the organ and played while I sang "How Great Thou Art." It's funny how death brings people together. By the time I'd finished singing, the whole place was crying, and so was I.

Tara Stiles broke the sad spell. "Daddy wouldn't like it if he caught us looking sad. He wanted us to rejoice because while he'll miss all of you, we believe he's with our mother, and he's not in pain anymore. After the service, my sister and I would like you to meet us at Aldo's for a celebration of Daddy's life."

Ms. Biggins hugged her sister and took the mic from her. "I want everyone to know we're holding another memorial service for those who couldn't be here today. Doctor Greely, do you want to tell them about it?"

"We've decided to offer the annual William Walker Boardly award in Duke's name to the student who best shows friendship and kindness to others. As you all know, Duke was a strong believer that kids should respect one another, and he hated bullying in any form."

Even though I felt lousy, I couldn't help but smile when Doc announced that LeBron would be the first recipient. Roy must have put the bug in Doc's ear, and the teachers probably made it unanimous.

Doc held up his hand to stop the applause. "If anyone wishes to help fund this annual award, please sign up after this service.

LeBron looked like he was in shock but said, "Thanks, I'll do my best to live up to it."

Officer Grady moved next to Doc. "A number of staff members, including teachers, aides, and the security force, have pledged contributions already. We've decided to invest the money to help pay college tuition when the winners need it."

As we filed into Aldo's Bar and Grill, Nonna spotted two tough guys in muscle shirts sitting on the steps smoking. "You guys had better check out soon. We're giving our friend a send-off today, so we'll need you to scram."

They looked at each other and then at Nonna. "Let's go, Pat," the one with no teeth said. "It doesn't pay to argue with this lady. I tried it once and she yanked my ear like Godzilla the nun did in grade school. Almost ripped it out of my head."

"I'm out of here," his friend said, and they took off like someone had set their butts on fire.

After everyone had gobbled up Aldo's special sausage and peppers casserole and homemade tiramisu, I knew it was time to carry out Duke's music requests. I flipped the switch, and everyone stopped talking and started clapping to the music of "School Days" by Chuck Berry.

I looked over at Duke's daughters to see if it was okay with them and saw that they were clapping too. After the song ended, Ms. Stiles said. "Daddy would have loved this. I see you're saving the best for last, Elliot."

I held up the old 45 record to show everyone.

Tara smiled. "You all know how Daddy was always humming that sixties hit, "The Duke of Earl," but you may not know why that song was special to him, so let me tell you. When he and Mom dated, he'd serenade her with that song. I'm told he had quite a voice in his day. That song became their song from then on. She always called him her Duke, and he called her his Duchess. He never forgot. That's why he asked us to play it today."

My hands shook as I set up the record. It was a little scratchy but it was the real thing.

Everyone from school hummed along with the music like Duke did when he walked the halls. Nonna and Armand got carried away and started singing the words, which they knew by heart. Dad threw them a nasty look, but they kept right on singing.

After I played the song, I gave Ms. Stiles back the record, and she put it in a special sleeve like it was pure gold.

~ * ~

The guests filed out to their cars in the sweet spring air. Ray and LeBron caught up to me, and we strolled back to my house. We scurried up to my room, past Dad and Nonna, and I locked the door.

Roy touched my arm. "Sorry about Duke, amigo. No one expected him to die this soon. He's the kind of guy you think will be around forever."

LeBron plunked down on my bed. "There would never be a right time to lose him. At least we got to know him. You can help make what he believed in about helping bullied kids a reality."

Roy offered me a stick of gum. "Have you thought about how you're going to make that happen?"

I didn't feel like talking, but this was important to me, especially now that Duke was gone. "One thing I know is I'd like to help kids who feel trapped because of bullying. I want to help them help themselves, but I want other kids to get involved too."

LeBron chimed in, which was only right, 'cause this was a team effort. "I think you're saying you want kids to have options, to have friends they can turn to when things get too hot to handle on their own."

"Yeah, like what you guys did for me."

"What we do for each other," Roy corrected me.

"We're with you all the way, man," LeBron said.

Roy gave me a thumbs up. "Anything you need to launch this, you can count on us."

"Oh, by the way, "LeBron said, "Ms. Stiles and her sister wanted you to have this." LeBron plunked a cardboard crate marked "Florida Oranges, the cure for whatever ails you," into my arms. It reminded me how Duke had tried everything to reverse his cancer and heart problems. Why couldn't something have worked?

I looked inside the crate. "It's his whole collection of doo wop songs from the fifties and sixties."

Roy ruffled through the old records and tapes. "These could be worth money, El."

"I'd never sell them. Listening to these songs will help me connect with who he was before I met him."

"You're right," LeBron said. "This is vintage stuff, valuable in terms of Duke's history."

Suddenly a light went off in my head. "Maybe we can play these at the meetings of our Bullies Anonymous club, you know, as background music, so we can all remember who gave us the idea in the first place."

I chose a 45 record at random and set up Dad's old-fashioned record player. When I showed Roy and LeBron the record I'd grabbed, they couldn't believe it.

"You must have peeked," Roy said.

LeBron smiled. "Either that or Duke's spirit told you to pick it."

Gene Chandler could have been right in the room with his silk top hat and cape, waving the baton like he always did when he performed his oldies song, "The Duke of Earl."

I opened my door wide and turned the music up full blast until it almost broke our eardrums. Duke's song traveled down into the reposing rooms and out through the open windows into the street. I knew it was a sign.

Chapter Twenty-one: Reality

After Duke's death, I threw myself into rehearsing for the show. We practiced six days a week, but I was glad because it kept me from thinking about everything that happened this year, including the episodes with Kyle, the hospital stay, the hearing, and losing Duke. I wanted to move forward, away from the pain of what happened, but I never wanted to forget Duke.

Why is it when you're waiting for something to happen, time creeps by like a caterpillar? Waiting for opening night was like that. When it finally came, my stomach started doing somersaults.

Tonight, now that Dad had totally gotten back into his good graces, Mario, the singing barber, was subbing for him as a people greeter at a memorial service so Dad could attend my show. Dad made him promise not to sing "Funiculi, Funicula" or any of the other goofy songs he was famous for.

"If you want me to work, I have to sing," Mario said.

"Okay, but maybe you could sing something more in keeping with the mood like "Amazing Grace" or "The Battle Hymn of the Republic." It was more of a plea than a command because Mario never took orders from anyone, least of all Dad.

Mario swore on his mother's grave and his cat's grave that he'd do nothing to disrespect the dead. After all, most of his relatives were dead, and who knew when he would go.

"It's a deal," Dad said. They shook on it, but I could tell he didn't trust Mario.

Opening night was here at last. The school orchestra tuned up and zoomed into a medley of songs from "Man of La Mancha." It always amazes me how the jumbled up, flat-sounding tune-up can magically change into perfectly pitched music.

I moved the curtain and looked out at the audience. From backstage, I could see a crowd of faces blurred from the fuzzy stage lights. I smelled the hot dogs and popcorn that the Home and School parents were selling outside the auditorium. The silence was so thick it sounded like an ocean's roar.

I felt jittery standing backstage by the curtain waiting to go on, but once the curtain opened, I felt relaxed and free.

The show starts out in a prison and Rosinante, this fake horse, showed up to carry me on my adventures. At one point in the scene, I had to flip back the horse's disguise and shout, "Reality."

I couldn't believe I was here after all that happened and that I was doing something that excited me. This was my reality, and I hoped to keep it that way.

At the end of the show, I sang my last note, the highest one, "to reach the unreachable *star...*" and prayed my voice wouldn't crack. Luckily, I hit the note and the crowd cheered.

The audience gave us a standing ovation and three curtain calls. I could hear Dad shouting "Bravo, bravo" above the crowd. Mom sat next to him, and they looked like they were having fun together. It was hard to tell with them.

Who knew what would happen once Mom moved back to Philly? When Duke died, she said it made her more determined than ever to do something to help people. The kind of life he led made her think of how she needed to start over, to stop living the "empty life" she was living, doing something she didn't really believe in. I guess Duke touched more people's lives than he could ever have imagined.

Nonna and Armand held hands when they weren't clapping. I couldn't believe that someday soon she would be Angela Carnucci

Cacciatucci. It sounded more like a fancy chicken dish at Marra's restaurant rather than my grandmother's name, but that was her choice, not mine.

Ms. Stiles and Ms. Biggins waved to me from their front row seats. They wore their best dresses and jewelry for the occasion. I knew Duke was there too. I could feel it.

Rosalie and I, Don Quixote and Aldonza, took our bows arm in arm. The crowd shouted *El-li-ot, El-li-ot,* but not like some kids did before when they made fun of me. They loved the show. I think they actually liked me.

After we changed from our costumes, I met Rosalie next to the statue of Ralph Bunche. She was wearing a black skirt and a yellow sweater and glowed like they'd just crowned her Miss America. "My dad brought his Chevy convertible. He'll drive us to the cast party."

"Sounds classier than my dad's dead wagon."

I sat down on the marble bench next to the statue. "There's something I want to ask you."

"What's that?" She settled in next to me and moved close so our arms were touching.

I smiled at her. A rush of strength and confidence raced through me. "Do you want to go to the freshman dance with me next month?"

"That would be fun," she said, and I really believed she meant it. She looked toward her Dad's car where a group of kids shouted for us to hurry up.

"Come on, we don't want to be late," she said. She latched onto my hand and we ran to the car.

~ * ~

When I got back to school on Monday, Ms. Begley told me Doc wanted to see me. He motioned for me to sit in front of a microphone on his desk that piped out announcements over the PA system. "Today's the perfect day to talk about your new club. Attendance is up because it's free pizza and ice cream day. Ready to roll?"

I nodded. For a brief moment, I wondered what everyone would think of what I was going to say. The whole school, including Kyle's friends, Rosalie, and all my teachers would hear my message.

The school board ended up expelling Kyle despite his apology. I guess, unlike most people around here, they could see through him. His friends would probably tell him about my idea when they visited him in military school. I wondered how he'd react to it. Did I really want to know?

I moved close to the mic and Doc flipped the switch that would connect me with the whole school. "My name is Elliot K. Carnucci. Some of you know me from Matheletes, chorus, and drama. Some of you have never met me. If you're interested in what I have to say, leave a note in Doc's mailbox, and I'll call you.

"I'm starting a club called Bullies Anonymous. If anyone has ever hurt you physically, called you names, or embarrassed you in front of other kids, you're invited to the first meeting at my house next Saturday morning.

"Some of you were never bullied, but you've seen other kids putting up with it and nobody helping them. You wonder what you can do to help. This club's for you too.

"Ms. Gonzales, the counselor, will run the first meeting with me. Me and my friends, Roy and LeBron, will help set guidelines. Sometimes we'll have guest speakers like social workers, teachers and parents. Other times, it will just be us helping each other, talking and solving problems as they come up.

"I hope to see a big crowd for our first meeting at the Carnucci Home for Funerals. If that spooks you out, good. I might even give you a tour of my house if you come on a regular basis."

After he shut down the mic, Doc shook my hand and broke out into a big smile. "Hearing you say those things to the students and thinking about how far you've come makes my day, Elliot. In fact, it gives me hope things will be better for all of us in the future."

"Thanks, Doc. I know they will." I traipsed off to homeroom, honestly believing they would be.

After school, Ms. Begley, my homeroom teacher, ran to catch up with me. "After your announcement, Ms. Williams gave me a letter to give you. I thought you'd want to read it right away so you could jump start your project."

As soon as I got home, I opened the letter that was on school stationary. Ms. Williams, my English teacher wrote:

Dear Elliot,

We want you to know we're all behind you one hundred percent on your project. We'll do whatever we can to help make it a success.

Dr. Greely is going to meet with all the department heads to discuss how we can plan lessons in our classes that will help make kids more aware of how bullying hurts and what kids can do to help one another if they witness bullying.

As staff members, we'll also try to be more aware of what goes on at school to ensure what happened to you doesn't happen to other kids.

Every teacher at Bunche signed the letter. The cafeteria ladies, Miss Mabel and her friend, Ms. Gladys, signed it, and so did Officer Grady and the security staff.

All the custodians signed it too. The new head custodian, Ms. Latisha wrote,

In hopes that the memory of our dear friend Will Boardly lives on and that his mission continues.

I was off to a running start.

The next day, Doc caught up with me after school. "My mailbox is overflowing with messages from students interested in your club. You've got a lot of phone calls to make. My secretary says she'll help, if you want."

"Thanks, Doc, but I've got it covered."

He gave me a thumbs up. "Break a leg."

I followed Doc to his office, reached into his mailbox for my messages, and stuffed them in my backpack.

The Bullied Anonymous Club was now officially up and running, a reality, thanks to Duke, my friends, and, of course, me, Elliot K. Carnucci, president.

About the Author

Catherine DePino has published 15 books about bullying, grammar/writing, spirituality, and women's issues. Her background includes a BS in English and Spanish education, a master's in English education, and a doctorate in Curriculum Theory and Development and Educational Administration from Temple University. The author worked for many years as a teacher, department head, and disciplinarian in the Philadelphia School District. After this, she worked at Temple as an adjunct assistant professor and student teaching supervisor. Catherine has also written articles for national magazines, including The Christian Science Monitor and The Writer. She holds membership in the Association of Children's Book Writers and Illustrators. Her self-help book, Fire Up Your Life in Retirement: 101 Ways for Women to Reinvent Themselves, recently appeared on the market. Cool Things to Do If a Bully's Bugging You, debuted in 2016. Visit her website and contact her at www.catherinedepino.com.

www.ingramcontent.com/pod-product-compliance
Lightning Source LLC
LaVergne TN
LVHW012104160826
845678LV00014B/2922